NIGHT OF THE
LIVING LAWN
ORNAMENTS

NIGHT OF THE LIVING LAWN ORNAMENTS

By Emily Ecton

ALADDIN PAPERBACKS
NEW YORK   LONDON   TORONTO   SYDNEY

ALADDIN PAPERBACKS
An imprint of Simon & Schuster Children's Publishing Division
1230 Avenue of the Americas, New York, NY 10020
Text copyright © 2009 by Emily Ecton
All rights reserved, including the right of reproduction in whole
or in part in any form.
ALADDIN PAPERBACKS and related logo are registered trademarks
of Simon & Schuster, Inc.
Designed by Lisa Vega
The text of this book was set in Bembo.
Manufactured in the United States of America
First Aladdin Paperbacks edition March 2009
10 9 8 7 6 5 4 3 2 1
Library of Congress Control Number 2008929039
ISBN-13: 978-14169-6451-3
ISBN-10: 1-4169-6451-7

To my grandparents, Hazel and Earl Diffrient, Evelyn Alvis,
and the silver fox himself, Tom Alvis

CHAPTER 1

WHEN I GOT UP THIS MORNING, THE LAST THING I expected to do was spend the day hiding in the tree with a lobotomized orange kangaroo toy. Heck, it wasn't even on my list of planned activities, and that just shows how much I know—it should have been smack dab in the number-one spot.

My big plan for the day was to get dressed, have a couple of Ho Hos, maybe spend a little time trying to convince our chronically depressed mutant Chihuahua Mr. Boots that life is worth living. You know, your basic stuff.

Tackling Bethany Burgess the first week of school? Not in the plan. Taking off down the street waving my orange lobotomized stuffed friend like a baton in a relay race? Nowhere in the plan. Doing all that in my ratty Wonder Woman sweatpants with the hole in the butt? So not in the plan.

It's all because of our old neighbors, the Knobles. They had to relocate to a more secure environment, as my mom likes to say, which is actually not so secret code for going to jail. It's not like I missed them—it's hard to get nostalgic for people who called my best friend Ty "my little black friend" to his face (which they totally did).

But two seconds after the new neighbors moved into the Knobles' house, my mom fell head over heels in love with their six-year-old daughter, Cookie. It's actually embarrassing. She calls Cookie the daughter she never had, which kind of ticks me and Tina off since we're the daughters she actually did have.

My treetop buddy, Mr. Lobotomy—as I now refer to

him—used to be Fred, my perfectly normal and beloved kangaroo toy, and if I didn't play with him as much as I used to, it might have something to do with the fact that I'm in freaking high school now. But Mom decided it was a sign that I don't appreciate and value my things, and gave Fred to Cookie. Which, okay, basically sucks, but I'm sure I would've gotten over it eventually. Or I would've if I hadn't walked outside and caught Cookie removing the inner workings of Fred's skull with a pair of pinking shears. Mom was standing right there too, talking to Cookie's Mom, Mrs. Big Cookie, as I like to think of her, and neither one of them lifted a finger to stop her. They thought it was cute.

I don't think my reaction was that unusual, considering. Screaming like a banshee, snatching what was left of Fred away from Cookie, and streaking down the sidewalk seems like a very reasonable response, in my opinion.

And, okay, grab-and-run isn't exactly the world's best plan. But I'm pretty sure things would've worked out in the long run. I would've apologized, bought the demon spawn a new toy, and all would have been forgiven and forgotten. It would've been fine if I hadn't proceeded to completely flatten Bethany Burgess as I made my escape.

Bethany Burgess is my sister Tina's new best friend and, just like Tina, she's one of those super-stylish girls who eat dorky girls like me for lunch without batting an eye. She's not the kind of girl you want to tick off. Definitely not the kind of girl you shove onto her butt while she's wearing new white capri pants. Not unless you're hoping to achieve instant outcast status in high school (which I was not).

So naturally, that's what I proceeded to do.

Once I'd flattened Bethany, I did a split-second assessment of the situation. I could already see the headlines in the town tabloid, the *Daily Squealer*—CRAZY WONDER WOMAN WANNABE WITH LOBOTOMIZED ORANGE SIDEKICK SACKS MISS POPULARITY, BECOMES INSTANT PARIAH. Not the kind of publicity I was hoping for after just one week in school. So I went with the only option I had left: hightail it out of there and hide in a tree until the whole thing blew over. I figured it would take forty to fifty years tops.

I leapfrogged over Bethany before she'd managed to get a punch in (and she's got a mean right hook too), jumped over Mr. Boots, who was staring off into space like a tiny hurdle in a daisy hat, and skittered around my best friend, Ty, who was gaping at me from across the street with a look of total horror on his face. Nice to know Ty has my back, that's all I can say there. That horrified look was real helpful. It basically convinced me that fifty years in a tree might not be long enough.

The tree I picked was two streets over, across from Mrs. Wombat's house, a choice that pretty much insured that I'd be spending my days lonely and alone. Because I can sure as heck guarantee that no one is going to be hanging around outside Mrs. Wombat's house. You can't—she calls the cops on you. And that's if you're lucky. According to the stories I've heard, her yard is littered with the bones of her many unfortunate victims.

Mr. Lobotomy glared at me from the branch next to mine. He didn't look pleased in the least.

"Hey, buddy, I'm not any happier about this than you are," I said. Although it's pretty much a given that I was happier. I wasn't the one with a wisp of my Poly-fil brain stuck to the gaping hole in my head.

I don't know how long we sat that way—once your butt starts hurting, every minute feels like an hour, so it's hard to judge. I had a good view of Mrs. Wombat's front yard, so I decided to do a little amateur spying to keep my mind off my serious case of branch butt. So far I hadn't spotted any bones anywhere. But Mrs. Wombat has a pretty extensive monitoring routine going on—every quarter hour on the dot she does a scan of the yard.

"I can bring supplies if you need them. Did you bring a can opener?"

Ty's voice surprised me so much, I almost fell out of the tree.

I clung to the limb in what I hoped was a casual way and glared down at him. "Took you long enough."

By my estimation, Ty should've shown up with supplies hours ago. I mean, seriously, he saw me run off. How many places could I have gone?

Ty waggled a limp Mr. Boots at me from under the tree. "Mr. Boots needed to get gussied up first."

I snorted. Once Mom stopped caring whether Mr. Boots went around nude or not, the poor dog pretty much lost all interest in everything, fashion included. It's like he doesn't even care anymore. Like right now—a daisy hat? With a purple faux-fur bolero jacket? And no pants? You think he's depressed now, wait till he's plastered all over *People*'s Worst Dressed issue in his flower show pimp outfit. And given the way the *Daily Squealer* follows him around, it's not like it couldn't happen.

"Somebody's missing his sister!" Ty waggled Mr. Boots at me again. Mr. Boots didn't even react—he just lolled his head to the side. He did look pretty ridiculous, but I wasn't in a mood to be cheered up.

7

"Ty, forget it, okay?" I geared up for a grouchy rant, but the sound of the screen door slamming across the street stopped me cold. I looked at my watch. A quarter after. Wombat time. We were so busted.

"Ty! Quick! Mrs. Wombat!"

Ty started to roll his eyes at me like Mrs. Wombat was no big deal, but let me tell you, the sound of a potato gun firing wipes the smirk off your face pretty fast.

"Heads up, Arlie!" Ty chucked Mr. Boots at me and hopped up into the tree before I'd even registered what was happening. Lucky for Mr. Boots, I've got pretty fast dog-catching reflexes. Not that he even seemed to care. I don't think his brush with danger even registered. I draped him over a forked branch in what I hoped was a comfortable sitting position and tried to look like a squirrel.

"I know you're out here," Mrs. Wombat yelled from across the street, reloading her potato gun. She had a whole sack of Yukon Golds on the stoop beside her. "I can smell you, delinquents! You better show yourself and skedaddle before the cops get here!"

"Think she knows where we are?" Ty breathed. His squirrel impression wasn't nearly as convincing as mine.

I shook my head. "And she won't come after us, even if she does. She might shoot us, but she won't leave the yard."

That's the good thing about eccentric neighbors: Once you figure out their quirks, they're pretty predictable. Mrs. Wombat, for instance, is (a) crazy as a loon; (b) very territorial; (c) pretty much housebound. I don't think I've ever seen her set foot off of her property.

I peeked through the branches to get a better look. It's hard to be intimidated by a five-foot-tall woman surrounded with woodland animal lawn decorations, but Mrs. Wombat manages to pull it off. Mom says that stuff about the bones is just talk. I sure hoped she was right.

Her real name isn't even Mrs. Wombat—it's Wombowski or something like that. But me and Ty always thought she looked like a wombat, so that's what we went with. (Later on, when I actually saw a picture of a wombat, I realized we'd been thinking of a badger, but by that time it was way too late to change our ways.)

"She's not seriously going to call the cops, right?" Ty apparently didn't have a clear view from his perch, otherwise he wouldn't ask. Mrs. Wombat is the only woman I know who can balance a potato gun, dial a cordless phone, and still look like she could reach down your throat and rip your insides out.

"Oh, she's calling, all right."

Ty swallowed and looked around. "They'll spot us for sure. Your toy's going to blow our cover."

Mr. Lobotomy glared at him, but it was true. He was way more orange than any kangaroo had a right to be. I wouldn't have been surprised to find out his mother had been a blaze orange hunting vest.

I cursed under my breath and crawled farther out on the branch to look down the street. I figured we had five, ten minutes tops to figure out a strategy. As soon as the squad cars showed up, it was all over. And it's not like we'd get any sympathy from them. Heck, Sheriff

Shifflett was the one who'd helped Mrs. Wombat make the potato gun in the first place, to keep her from peppering the neighborhood kids with buckshot. He thought it was a safe alternative. Fat lot he knew. Those potatoes leave a mark.

I leaned farther out on the branch, and my hand closed over something that was definitely not tree. Something metal was twisted in the branch, like a chain or something. I tried to pick the leaves away from it without blowing my cover.

"Huh." It wasn't easy to get a look at it and keep my balance at the same time. It was really thin and fine, not the kind of thing you expect to find in the wild. I couldn't figure it out. Because as far as I know, trees don't typically wear jewelry, and that's sure as heck what this seemed like.

I tried to untangle the metal to get whatever it was free when I heard them—sirens. "No, that's way too fast!" I groaned.

"Man, don't those cops have anything else to do?"

Ty muttered, and shot me a look. "It's now or never, Arlie."

I nodded and tugged at the chain one last time. It broke and came off in my hand. I slipped the chain into Mr. Lobotomy's empty head as Ty grabbed Mr. Boots. Then I gritted my teeth and got ready to skedaddle.

"At the count of three," Ty said, and then he jumped.

"Count of three means counting, Ty!" I hissed as I jumped after him, doing my best to avoid breaking my neck on the sidewalk. Remind me to give Ty a basic tutorial in escaping etiquette.

Ty must've hit the ground running, because he was half a block ahead of me by the time I'd scrambled to my feet and taken off after him. Mrs. Wombat screeched in rage and let a warning shot loose in the sky (at least I'm hoping it was a warning shot. I'd hate to think she'd really take a potshot at a ninth grader in Wonder Woman sweatpants).

It was actually kind of exciting, like we were spies

running away with a huge fireball behind us, except less cool and with no fireball. I lost a flip-flop in our escape, but I really doubt it's enough to incriminate me. It's not like I was going back for it. I didn't stop until I'd caught up with Ty two blocks from the Happy Mart.

"Any tatershot in your butt?" Ty panted, leaning over with his hands on his knees.

I shook my head and flopped down next to Mr. Boots, who was sprawled out on the sidewalk, completely unfazed. Apparently doggie pimps elude danger every day and it's the most boring thing ever.

"Terrific." Ty grinned at me. "This calls for a Happy Dog."

"If you're buying." I pointed to my sweatpants. "I think my wallet's in my other pants."

"Mooch." Ty slapped me on the back.

I chucked Mr. Lobotomy into the grass beside me and he toppled over onto his side, spilling the chain out of his head. I scooted him back so I could see what kind of new brains I'd set him up with. And when I did, I could almost feel my eyes bugging out of my head.

I don't know what I'd expected, but whatever it was, it wasn't this. That wasn't just some kid's cheap Hello Kitty necklace. Lying in the dust next to Mr. Lobotomy's head was a sparkling black dragonfly pendant—definitely antique and definitely expensive. And definitely not mine.

CHAPTER 2

I'M PRETTY SURE I DID YOUR TYPICAL CARTOON reaction: exaggerated double take, eyes bulging out, that kind of thing. The only thing that was missing was the wacky *ow-OO-gah* sound effect. I slowly reached out and poked the dragonfly with one finger. It was so black that it seemed to absorb the light, but the edges sparkled in the sun. I'd never seen anything like it before, not even on the Home Shopping Network.

Ty stopped huffing and stretching his hamstrings and did a double take. "Holy cow, Arlie, what's that?"

"It was in the tree."

Ty gave me a new freakout look of horror. Seriously, those were starting to get old. "You mean you stole it?"

Geez, way to exaggerate the situation. "No, Ty. I didn't steal it. It was in the tree, okay? It didn't belong to anybody. Unless you count the tree, in which case, yeah, I totally stole it. The shrub Mafia's going to be after me, so watch out."

Ty took a closer look at the pendant and did his best to whistle. Unsuccessfully, as usual. "That thing's expensive, Arlie. It definitely belongs to someone. They're going to want it back. It was just sitting in the tree?"

I wiped the spit off of my face and glared at him. "See this chain? It was twisted around the branch and it's seriously messed up. It looks like it'd been there for years."

Ty squinted at me. "It's not cursed, is it?"

I groaned. "Geez, Ty, does it look cursed? Not everything is cursed, okay?" I sure hoped it wasn't cursed.

Although with our track record, I could see why he'd say that. If anyone was going to find a cursed dragonfly pendant, it would be us.

Ty perked up. "So what you're saying is, it's abandoned? Like buried treasure?"

That wasn't exactly what I was thinking, but sure, okay. I nodded.

"It's up for grabs then? Sweet!" Ty grabbed the dragonfly and draped it around his neck. "So, tell me the truth, is it me?"

In a word, no. Even Mr. Boots snickered, and he was practically comatose.

"Yeah, nice try." I reached out to take the dragonfly pendant back, but Ty was too quick for me.

He draped it dramatically around the neck of a garden gnome in the yard next to us. "So it's more a gnome kind of thing, you think?"

He stood back and examined the gnome critically. "Nope, definitely not right for this guy. Maybe this guy?" He looped the necklace over the beak of a pink flamingo standing nearby, and then when that didn't meet with his approval, over the beak of another flamingo, two more gnomes, and a couple of posing happy squirrels. It was cute at first, but come on, how long does it take to figure out that ancient black dragonfly pendants are unflattering to the majority of your common garden decorations? And with all the crap people in this town keep on their lawns, if Ty went through every one, we'd be there for weeks.

"Cut it out, Ty." I tried to smack the plastic garden penguin he was holding out of his hand, but all I managed to do was bruise my thumb. I glared at the penguin. Like penguins even live in gardens. "We didn't steal it, but I don't know how we're going to explain it either. Do you want to try to explain it to Shifflett?"

Let's just say that Sheriff Buck Shifflett isn't that fond of me and Ty. We generally try to stay out of his way. Unsuccessfully, unfortunately. But we'd managed to steer clear of him for over a month now, and I didn't want to mess that up.

Ty nodded and unlooped the dragonfly pendant from around the penguin's neck. "Good point. Doesn't really go with his suit, anyway. Happy Dogs then?"

I grinned and held out Mr. Lobotomy. I figured he wouldn't really mind if I used his head as a carrying case. It wasn't like he was using it for much anymore. Ty dangled the dragonfly over Mr. Lobotomy's skull and, just as he was about to let go, he got that whacked-out *I'm a lunatic* look in his eyes. I'm serious, you could practically see the lightbulb go off in his head, it was that obvious. And the pathetic thing is, I knew exactly what he was thinking.

"Forget it, Ty." He was going to get us so busted. I was beginning to hope that pendant did belong to the tree—at least a tree can't press charges for grand larceny.

"Just one more, okay?" Ty took off in the direction of the Happy Mart. "This'll be awesome!" he called back over his shoulder.

I scooped Mr. Boots up by the hind legs and draped him over my shoulder. It didn't take a brain surgeon to figure out where Ty was going. He was heading for the Happy Hog.

The Happy Hog is kind of a local mascot—it's this giant seven-foot-tall hog statue wearing a chef's hat, blue vest, and no pants. Pretty much the same look Mr. Boots was going with today, now that I thought about it. By the time I got over to the Hog, Ty had already worked his fashion magic and was standing back, rubbing his chin with his hand in an appraising way.

"Now, I don't know, Arlie. The cravat?" He waved his hand at the Happy Hog, who was now sporting an ancient dragonfly pendant in his neckerchief.

"Or, the more modern look?" Ty grabbed the pendant, did some adjusting, and stepped back to reveal the Happy Hog now sporting a fairly realistic looking dragonfly nose ring.

I groaned and shook my head. "You're sick, Ty. You know that?" I tried to shift Mr. Boots, but I think he'd surgically implanted his claws into my shoulder.

Ty grinned. "You just don't appreciate my genius."

Mr. Boots definitely snickered at that one. I decided to ignore it. "Happy Dog?"

Ty rolled his eyes at me. "You're no fun, Arlie." He retrieved the dragonfly pendant and stuffed it back into Mr. Lobotomy's head.

"There she is!"

I froze. Even from a couple of blocks away, there was no mistaking that voice. I should've stuck to my original plan and stayed in the tree for fifty years. At least that way, Bethany Burgess and my sister, Tina, wouldn't have found me.

I'd caught a glimpse of Tina's face as I ran away like a freak earlier, and I knew I was in deep with her. Her life had been pretty close to perfect lately—she'd gotten Miss Popularity for a new best friend, she was going out with the supercute new deputy sheriff, and she was coming into the new year as the reigning Prom Queen. Believe me, anybody who messes things up for her is going to be toast. And I have to admit, I was feeling pretty crispy at the moment.

I ducked down behind the Happy Hog like I was suddenly extremely interested in the intricacies of the Happy Hog's rear.

"Shoot, Ty. Is it clear? Can I make a run for it?" I whispered desperately. My only chance was to lay low until Tina cooled off.

Tina's voice seemed to have flipped Mr. Boots's on switch, because he suddenly started swiveling his huge bat ears around like satellite dishes looking for a signal. I couldn't hear anything, though, except the bell jingling on the Happy Mart door. I needed serious help here. I whacked Ty on the shin. "Ty! Which way?"

At first I thought he hadn't even heard me, but then without warning he dropped down and huddled next to me behind the Happy Hog's bulbous butt. "Shut up, Arlie. Just stay quiet, okay?" he hissed.

Me and Mr. Boots exchanged confused looks. Unless Ty had done something I wasn't aware of, which, to be fair, was entirely possible, he wasn't on Tina's current hit list. So I didn't get his whole duck-and-cover routine.

I peeked around the edge of the Hog's butt to do a quick Tina scan, but a pair of purple baggy knees blocked my view.

"Meet you at your place," Ty squeaked, and shot off down the street.

I groaned. We're talking great friend here, right? That's pretty much a signature Ty move, ditching me in my time of need. He even took Mr. Lobotomy and the dragonfly pendant with him.

"Was that Tyrone Parker?" The girl attached to the baggy knees was using such a sugary sweet voice, it made my teeth hurt.

I peered up at her, but it's not easy to make an ID when you're basically looking up someone's nostrils. The purple Crocs and pilled-up tights weren't telling me much, except that we had a severe fashion victim here. And when Arlie Jacobs can tell you've got fashion issues, you know it's extra bad.

"Who wants to know?" I wasn't giving out information to just anyone.

"Arlie, it's Christie, dummy."

I squinted up at her again, and it clicked. Christie O'Dell. She's a couple of years younger than me and Ty, and I've seen her around town. Actually, she's been around a lot lately, now that I think about it, but that doesn't explain why Ty took off as soon as her purple Crocs made an appearance.

"Don't worry, Bethany, she's going to pay for those pants." Tina's voice was a lot closer now.

"Damn straight," Bethany huffed.

Did I mention that I'm not one of Bethany's favorite people?

Mr. Boots swiveled his ears into position and shrank further down into his faux-fur jacket.

There was nothing to be done but ditch and run. "Sorry, gotta go." I shot an apologetic look at Christie (or, technically, Christie's leg) and scurried away as fast as humanly possible while crouching and carrying a tiny canine pimp. I just hoped that Hog's butt was big enough to cover our escape.

I took off for home the long way and did a couple of reconnaissance sweeps around the house to make sure no one was home before meeting Ty. He was sitting on our back porch, listlessly dangling the dragonfly pendant over Mr. Lobotomy's head. He didn't even look up when I walked over.

I'd managed to put a couple of things together on the way home, but it still wasn't adding up. "Tell me the truth. Were you seriously running away from CHRISTIE?" Tina, I could understand. Tina on the warpath meant certain doom. But a seventh grader in purple Crocs? Please. Her picture's in the dictionary under "not scary."

Ty scowled at me and spat in the dirt. You know, because that's shorthand for cool. Mr. Boots and I were not impressed.

"Drop it, Arlie. Here's your toy." He dropped the necklace into Mr. Lobotomy's head and handed him to me without another word. Then he sauntered off down the street for a few feet before taking off running.

Mr. Boots stared after him for a second and then raised his eyebrows at me. I shrugged and headed inside. If I'd known when I got up how much this day was going to suck, I would've just stayed inside and left Mr. Lobotomy to his fate. It's not like I did him much good, anyway.

I figured once I'd made it safely to my room, I'd be home free. Plus I needed some alone time for strategizing if I was going to get out of this mess.

I chucked Mr. Boots on my bed and made sure my door was locked before I took out the dragonfly pendant. It sparkled in my hand. I shivered. As pretty as it was, that thing was giving me the creeps. I know that sounds paranoid, but given the year I've had, being paranoid seems like a pretty good daily strategy.

I tried to shrug it off, though. It was just a necklace, right? And unless there's some evil warlock of Zales that I'm unfamiliar with, necklaces are generally pretty safe things.

Mr. Boots had flopped back on my pillows and was

staring at the ceiling like he was settling in for his daily therapy session. And for some reason, that made me go into silly mode. I'd had a rough day. So sue me.

I picked up Mr. Boots's favorite squeaky bunny from the floor and draped the dragonfly around the bunny's neck.

"So tell me, Boots, how does that make you feel?" I tried to give the bunny squeaky a fake German accent, but even alone in my room I cringed at how lame I sounded. It's pretty bad when you're embarrassing even to yourself. Mr. Boots just curled his lip at me.

The dragonfly was looking kind of grubby, but not much looks good nestled in matted faux-sheepskin, so I took it off of the squeaky bunny and headed downstairs.

I tested the dragonfly around the neck of the Egyptian cat statue my mom has in the entryway and stepped back. Definitely grubby. It didn't look any better on the china dog on the mantel.

I figured if I worked fast, I could clean it up before

Tina got home, so I hustled into the kitchen. I needed a cover story in case anyone came in, though, so I pulled the pepper canister out and uncorked Mom's sheep-shaped pepper shaker. I figured I could pretend to be filling it if I got caught. Then I got to work on the dragonfly with Mom's organic banana jewelry cleaner.

Thank goodness I'd thought of the pepper shaker cover, because I'd barely gotten one wing clean when I heard the front door slam. I stuffed the dragonfly into the sheep shaker just as Tina shot into the kitchen like a ballistic missile of rage. Lucky for me, Mom was right behind her. And as mad as Tina was, it's hard to kill your sister when your mom's in the room. Even so, Tina had me by the collar by the time Mom had caught up.

"There you are, young lady." Mom was in her angry mode, with steam practically coming out of her nostrils. But even on her worst day, she's an angel compared to Tina. I scooted the sheep-shaped pepper shaker behind me to make it less noticeable and tried to look cute and apologetic.

Tina pulled me so close that I could smell her lip gloss. "You are so dead, Arlie. You're going to pay for what you did to Bethany." Man, you'd think I'd stolen her firstborn instead of just getting grass stains on her capris. But it didn't matter. I closed my eyes. As innocent and pretty as Tina looks, she doesn't make idle threats. I was doomed.

Thankfully, Mom came to my rescue.

"Now, Tina, let me handle this, okay?" Mom put her hand on Tina's shoulder and pulled her back. It took some pulling to get Tina's hands to unclench from my collar, but she finally let go. "Now, Arlie, you are going to apologize to Cookie. You are going to apologize to Mrs. Saunders. And you are going to apologize to Bethany. Maybe pay for her pants."

It took a minute for it to click with me that Mrs. Saunders was Mrs. Big Cookie, but I was already yessing and nodding my head off. Heck, if it would get Tina off my back, I'd apologize to half the free world. I'd apologize to Christie for mentally mocking her baggy knees and to the Happy Hog for crouching disrespect-fully behind his butt. I'm not even kidding here.

"I don't have to tell you how disappointed I am in you. I have an early morning meeting tomorrow, and when I get back, I want to hear that you've made amends. Now Tina, come with me. Arlie, you go to your room and think about what you've done."

Tina narrowed her eyes at me. I could tell she didn't want to let me off that easy, but there wasn't much she could do. Mom was sure to notice a black eye or two at this point.

I waited until they left the room, shook the pendant out of the sheep-shaped pepper shaker, and headed up to my room for some serious thinking about what I'd done/alone time.

I couldn't help but smile with relief, though. The worst was over. Apologizing and groveling wouldn't be that bad. Yeah, today stunk, but tomorrow would be fine. At least that's what I thought then. Until the next morning, when the screaming started.

CHAPTER 3

BELIEVE ME, WAKING UP TO BLOODCURDLING shrieks isn't one of my top-ten preferred ways to wake up in the morning. I shot out of bed so fast, I hit my head on the door frame, staggered down the hall, and just missed taking a header down the stairs. I don't even know what I was thinking—a Mr. Boots mishap with the electric can opener, maybe? Garbage disposal accident? Not that those even made any sense, but I was expecting blood, and lots of it.

I wasn't expecting to find a sheep-shaped

pepper shaker wailing and spewing pepper out of its nostrils all over the counter.

"Harold!" the pepper shaker wailed. It was clutching the salt shaker and shaking it furiously. "Speak to me!"

I'll admit it, I didn't really know how to react. I just kind of stood there with my mouth hanging open. There's not a lot to say in that situation.

The pepper shaker noticed me and glared.

"You, there, with the duck on your shirt, help me!" the pepper shaker shrieked, sneezing and wiping its nose with its hoof. "DO something! What's WRONG with him?"

"Uh," I said. Yes, great moments in the life of Arlene Jacobs. "I, uh . . ."

"He won't say ANYTHING!" the pepper shaker wailed again. "Is he mad at me?"

I shrugged in what I hoped was a sympathetic way and tried to assess the situation. I was pretty sure I wasn't dreaming, because I could hear Mom's hair dryer going upstairs, and that's not the kind of detail I usually include in my dreams. Which meant this was either really happening or I was hallucinating. Neither option was good.

"What do you want him to say? Did . . . uh . . . did you two have a fight?" I said, edging back toward the door. I'll admit it—I was planning to make a break for it. And I probably would've made it if I hadn't heard Tina's feet galumphing down the stairs.

"What's that?" the pepper shaker said, cocking its head in a listening pose. "Dragon? Elephant?"

Tina as a fire-breathing dragon was a pretty good description, actually. I was half hoping for a real dragon, though, because the last thing I wanted was for Tina to meet my new pepper shaker friend. I shot across the kitchen, covered the pepper shaker's mouth with my hand, and hid it behind my back.

Tina lurched into the kitchen and looked around suspiciously. "What the hell, Arlie? What's with the screaming? I was sleeping."

I gave an apologetic smile. "Sorry about that. I stubbed my toe."

Tina crossed her arms. "That was because you stubbed your toe? That's the noise you make? I hate to think what you're going to do when you feel some real pain."

Oh great, threats first thing in the morning, another perfect way to start the day. If I thought I could get away with it, I'd go back upstairs and pretend I had the flu, maybe chalk ninth grade up as a complete loss.

The pepper shaker was not happy about being grabbed, I could tell. It squirmed in my hand and I could feel its tiny porcelain teeth biting at my finger. "Sorry about that. Go back to sleep."

Tina looked at her watch. "Forget it. Thanks to you, it's time for me to get up." She turned around and huffed upstairs. Tina has a pretty extensive morning makeup routine.

I slumped over the counter in relief and put the pepper shaker down on the cabinet.

"Don't you EVER do that to me again." The pepper shaker was shaking with rage. A dribble of pepper was coming out of its left nostril. "That was completely uncalled for."

"Sorry." I was definitely voting for hallucination at this point. I mean, I'd peppered my eggs with this thing for years, and now it was screeching at me. It was hard to do anything but blink at it.

Music started blasting from Tina's room, so the morning routine had definitely started. It was so loud that I almost didn't hear Mom's high heels on the stairs.

"Sorry in advance," I hissed, scooping the pepper shaker back up and planting my finger firmly over its mouth.

"Arlie, now don't forget what I said, okay?" Mom trotted into the kitchen, putting on her earrings.

This was not good.

"Apologies go a long way. Now when you get home from school, we'll talk, okay? And I want to hear how it went."

Mom came over and kissed me on the forehead. I felt the tiny porcelain teeth clamp down on the fleshy part of my finger. That sheep wasn't messing around this time. My eyes started watering, but I tried to ignore it.

Mom picked her purse up from the table and fished out her keys. An Egyptian-looking black cat wandered in from the living room, sat down behind Mom, and started grooming itself. Mom didn't notice. Which is good, because we don't have a black cat.

"Have a good day, Arlie. And try to stay out of trouble?" Mom smiled at me as she headed out the door.

I gave her a weak smile and held it until the door was completely shut. Then I put the pepper shaker down as fast as I could.

"Sheesh, cut it with the teeth, okay?" I scowled and inspected my finger. That thing had left a mark.

"No touching, okay?" The pepper shaker shook its hoof at me and then pointed at the salt shaker. "Is that what happened to him? Did you do that to Harold? Did you suffocate him with your grabby hands?"

I gaped at the pepper shaker. "What? No! I—" I

don't even know what I would've said. I mean, how do you defend yourself against the accusations of a hysterical pepper shaker? But whatever I was going to say was interrupted by a horrible scream from upstairs.

"Oh, no." I grabbed the pepper shaker and lurched upstairs and into my room.

"Grabby hands! Grabby hands!" the pepper shaker shrieked. I just hoped that Tina couldn't hear anything over that music of hers.

Mr. Boots was in the corner, trying to spackle himself to the wall, it looked like. His eyes were glued to something small and orange in the middle of my floor. Something standing in front of my full-length mirror shrieking. Mr. Lobotomy.

"What happened to my HEAD?" he shrieked, waving his tiny orange paws around in the vicinity of his scalp. "Do you see this? This isn't the way it used to be! There never used to be a gaping hole in my head!"

"Fred?" I gasped, trying not to stare. But let me

tell you, that's not easy when your orange lobotomized stuffed toy is screaming at his reflection in your mirror. I don't know how many years of therapy it takes to fix something like that.

"Fred? Fred? Do I look like a Fred to you?" Fred whirled to face me, hands on his hips.

I didn't know what to say. Yes? I had just one goal in mind, which was, basically, don't piss off the stuffed toy.

"Fred's a boy's name. Do I look like I boy?" Apparently I didn't answer quickly enough because Fred tapped her foot angrily. "The answer is no, okay? No, I don't. I'm a girl."

"Well, yeah, sure, I know that," I bluffed, even though I totally didn't. How can you tell with stuffed toys? "Fred's just a nickname. Short for . . . for Frederika. That's what I figured, right?"

Fred huffed angrily, but seemed appeased. "Oh. Well, okay."

"A term of endearment, right?" the pepper shaker

said, dangling from my hand like it was on an amusement park ride.

"What the hell is that?" Fred said, eyeing the pepper
shaker warily.

The pepper shaker snorted, and puffs of pepper
floated around the room. "Excuse me?" It sneezed and
looked offended.

I put the shaker down onto the floor near Fred and
backed away. "Why don't you guys get acquainted."

The shaker snorted again. I was going to have a ton
of cleaning to do when this was all done. There was pepper all over the place.

Fred seemed to have already forgotten about the pepper shaker—I guess short-term-memory issues are pretty
much inevitable when you have no brain. She was peer-
ing into the closet intently.

"Hey, what's that—are those clothes?"

I glanced back at Mr. Boots. He shot me a look of
agony and started shaking, totally blowing his cover as
spackle. I really felt for the guy.

"Yeah, but they belong to Mr. Boots, so they're off limits." Add that to the list of rules I never thought I'd have to make.

"Oooh, fresh duds, sign me up." Fred waddled into the closet, opening and closing her tiny fists as she went.

I scooped Mr. Boots up and backed out of the room, carefully closing the door behind me. "Sorry, buddy. I tried." This was not good.

I took the stairs two at a time. Ty had to see this. Or, if there was nothing to see and I was really going crazy, I would need someone to wipe the drool off of my chin. Either way, he needed to get his butt over here.

Mr. Boots shrank back against me, shivering uncontrollably. As much as I'd like to think I'd just gone completely loony, I was beginning to think this wasn't a hallucination. Me and Mr. Boots are pretty close, but sharing hallucinations? We're not that close.

Tina had migrated downstairs into the living room and was watching TV and brushing her teeth. She spat into the glass she was holding and held it up to me like she was toasting me. It was then that I recognized it as my rinsing glass. I made a mental note to sabotage her toothbrush later on.

I scowled at her and picked up the cordless.

"Check this out, Arlie." She waved her toothbrush at the TV. I glanced at it. Not to be mean, but I had more important things to deal with than the weather forecast, okay? Namely, some cranky inanimate objects taking over my room. But like I could say that, right?

"Yeah, that's great," I said, barely looking at the set. But the picture on the screen looked awfully familiar. I stopped dialing and took a closer look at the TV. "What is that, downtown?"

Tina nodded. "The Happy Mart."

I felt my stomach go plummeting down through my feet and bounce on the basement floor. "What's wrong with the Happy Mart?" I tried to sound chipper, but I had a horrible feeling I already knew.

"It's not the Happy Mart," Tina said through a mouth full of toothpaste foam. "It's the Happy Hog. It's gone."

CHAPTER 4

I'M THINKING TY MUST BE PART SNAIL, BECAUSE it took him forever to get his butt over to my house. You'd think the words "angry pepper shaker," "Fred's come to life," and "missing Happy Hog" would light a fire under a person and make them hustle, but apparently, you'd be thinking wrong.

And also, according to some people, I'm prone to exaggeration and not to be taken seriously.

"Now what happened exactly? You thought

you saw the salt shaker move?" Ty glanced around the kitchen nonchalantly.

"It was the pepper shaker, and it was more like screaming and hysterical sobbing, thank you very much." I smiled grimly. Ty was in for a rude awakening, and I was glad to have a front-row seat.

"The pepper shaker." Ty put on his most understanding face, the one you use for crazy people and clueless check-out clerks. "Like this one?" He picked up the salt shaker and inspected it in a way that would've made the pepper shaker upstairs blush.

"Well, yeah, except that one is standing on four feet, and the pepper shaker always stands on two feet, in a more jaunty pose."

Ty just stared at me. "Jaunty. Got it."

"Plus, that one's not crying and puffing pepper clouds all over the place."

"Uh-huh." Ty looked like he was ready to whip out the straitjacket and haul me off to the rubber room. Which

I thought was pretty unfair considering the things we've been through. I mean, give me some credit, right?

I rolled my eyes. "Just, come on. They're upstairs." I could hear giggling coming from my room. I'm glad someone was having a good time.

Mr. Boots eyed us as we went past. Through some amazing feat of climbing, he seemed to have taken up residence on top of the refrigerator. I didn't blame him.

Ty headed on upstairs with his newly acquired world-weary attitude. One week of high school and already he knows it all.

"Don't let him push you around, toots. You show him what's what."

I hung back and peered into the living room, trying to figure out who had decided to become my personal cheerleader. The china dog on the mantel gave me the thumbs-up.

"Great." I sighed. I was surprised I wasn't more shocked. "You want to go upstairs too?"

"Sounds good to me, you bet." At least the china

dog wasn't wailing and crying. I'd had enough of knick-knack angst for one day.

I got upstairs with the china dog just as Ty opened my bedroom door. I thought he was going to head inside, but he seemed to stall just inside the doorway. One look at his face told me why. I forced myself not to grin. It was a long time coming, but it looked like the freak-out was finally here. It's hard to maintain the world-weary pose when you're confronted with a knickknack jamboree. I peeked around him to see what was going on inside the room.

Fred was wearing one of Mr. Boots's prairie bonnets (which was a good move on her part, because it totally hid the huge hole in her head) and was modeling the matching blue pinafore for the pepper shaker. I'm glad Mr. Boots wasn't here to see it. He loved that outfit.

"I don't know." Fred craned her head around to get a better look in the mirror. "Does this dress make my butt look big?"

"I think it's the way it's cut. It makes you look hippy."

The pepper shaker wiped her nose. Little trickles of pepper leaked out from around her hoof.

"He's a kangaroo. Kangaroos are hippy," the china dog piped up as I put him down onto the carpet.

Ty made a couple of mouth motions like he was planning on talking, but no words came out, just little puffs of air. I patted him on the shoulder. It was a lot to take in.

"*She!* I'm a *girl*! And I am not hippy!" Fred looked indignant.

"What? It's a fact. Kangaroo equals hippy. Look it up!" The china dog rolled his eyes.

"Of course you're not hippy." The pepper shaker glared at the dog and sneezed.

I hoped I wasn't going to have to split them up. When everybody's made of porcelain, even a slap-fight can get ugly fast.

Ty grabbed my arm and dragged me out of the room, closing the door behind me. "Arlie, this is not good. They're talking. We are in so much trouble."

"What, you're keeping secrets now?" that china dog yelled through the door. No wonder Mom kept it stashed way back on the mantel.

"It's that dragonfly. It was cursed, wasn't it?" Ty whisper yelled at me. "I knew we should've just left it alone."

I smacked him on the arm. "Cut it out—there is no curse. Way to jump to conclusions." Of course it made perfect sense. That dragonfly had touched everything that was alive right now. But in my experience, curses come neatly labeled with the word "curse" attached just so there's no confusion, and this was just a necklace in a tree. And there was no way I was going to claim responsibility for the angry knickknacks currently trashing my room, thank you very much.

"You're telling me the dragonfly didn't do this? Your pepper shaker issues? The Happy Hog? That doesn't sound like a curse to you? Come on, Arlie, put two and two together."

"There's nothing that says we did this, Ty. It's not

our fault. And, besides, you didn't seem to be worrying about curses when you were slinging the dragonfly all over town," I said in my cold and frosty voice.

I turned my back on Ty, opened the door, and gave my best cheery smile. "No secrets!"

"Did you touch those things with the dragonfly?" Ty demanded.

"Well, yeah. But that doesn't mean anything." I know, super convincing.

Ty staggered across the room and threw open the window to get some air. I didn't say anything, but he really needed to be more careful where he stepped. One inch to the left and our china dog friend would be missing a backside right now. I'm just saying.

I headed over to Ty and happened to glance out of the window, and what I saw outside made me feel like doing a happy dance. Mom's garden gnomes were going to town—doing some hedge trimming, a little edgework, just your basic lawn activities. I grabbed Ty by the arm triumphantly. "See those gnomes, Ty? I didn't touch those gnomes. Not a single one. So it's definitely not us."

Ty didn't say anything, he just scuffed the carpet with the toe of his shoe.

"What?" I didn't like the way his face was getting that rosy glow of guilt. "I didn't, okay? Maybe I touched the other things, but not a single gnome. So I'm thinking it's something in the water? Maybe another chemical spill?" The chemical plant was always causing problems, so I figured they were a good candidate for this kind of thing.

Ty cleared his throat. "I may have, uh . . . touched a couple of them. You know. With the necklace."

My stomach, which I'd already left in the basement, started tunneling for the center of the earth. "You did."

"Yeah." Ty wouldn't meet my eye.

"Which ones?"

"Maybe all of them?"

"Geez, Ty! What, did everything between here and the Happy Mart get a personal Ty makeover session?"

Leave it to Ty to totally ruin my illusion of innocence.

"Well, how was I supposed to know? It was funny!" Ty shot me an angry look. I ignored it and turned back to the knickknack costume fitting, which was still in full swing.

"I don't know if pink's my color." Fred was modeling one of Mr. Boots's pink party dresses and twirling his pink parasol now (which was fine by me, because Mr. Boots had never really gotten the hang of the whole parasol thing).

"Definitely the blue. Better for your skin tone." The pepper shaker nodded.

"Uh, excuse me," I interrupted. Fred and the pepper shaker both glared at me. The china dog just snickered.

"Fred, if you don't mind, I think you have a necklace in your head?"

Fred shot the pepper shaker a sidelong glance. The pepper shaker looked at the carpet, like it was trying to spare Fred an embarrassing moment. "Yeah? So?"

"Could I have that for a minute please?"

"Yeah, I don't think so." Fred held up the blue dress again.

Ty elbowed me in the ribs. I think it left a mark. "Arlie, what are you doing?"

"We're going to test it out, okay? We'll see once and for all whether that dragonfly is bringing things to life."

Ty stared at me like I'd just hopped on the crazy train. "Not a good idea, okay? That's the last thing we need to do."

"Just one more thing. That shaker there."

I pointed to Ty's hand, where he was still holding the salt shaker loosely.

"HAROLD!" the pepper shaker shrieked. "Be careful with him!" The shaker rushed Ty and started jumping up and down, like it was going to be able to rescue the salt shaker.

Ty looked at his hand guiltily and then put the salt shaker down on the rug. "Sorry about that."

The pepper shaker draped itself dramatically around the salt shaker and started sniveling. I was definitely going to have some vacuuming to do in the near future.

"Come on, Fred. Please? We need to do a test."

Fred narrowed her eyes and me and glared. "Nobody's going inside my head. Got it?"

"Please, Fred. Do it for Harold!" The pepper shaker's lip was quivering and everything. Even Fred couldn't resist a display like that. After all, she wasn't made of stone.

"Well, okay, fine. But nobody's touching this head but me. Got it?" Fred undid her bonnet. "Now everybody look away. And no peeking."

We all covered our eyes and waited while Fred rooted around in her skull and came out with the dragonfly pendant. (Okay, I'll confess. I peeked.)

"Now what?" Fred held the pendant out to me.

"Maybe just put it inside? That's probably the best bet," Ty suggested.

Right away I knew we had a problem. I've been using those shakers for years and let me just say that I know where the stopper is.

"Oh, no. No no, you don't. Oh no, thank you, Mister.

No way, no how." The pepper shaker started shaking and puffing like crazy, trying to protect the salt shaker's hindquarters and cover her own at the same time. "Nobody's messing with our stoppers, got it?"

"Calm down," I said. It was like I was talking the shaker back from the edge of a ledge, that's how riled up she was. "Nobody's messing with anyone's stopper, okay? We'll just drape it over his head here."

I draped the dragonfly over Harold's neck and backed away.

"Stopper would've been better," Ty grumbled, but Fred shut him up with a quick glare.

Once the dragonfly was in place, we all sat back and watched. And waited. And waited some more.

It got pretty boring actually. I heard the door slam as Tina left for school. If something didn't happen soon, me and Ty were going to be really late for homeroom. But with each minute that passed, my insides unclenched a little bit. Because if Harold didn't come to life, that meant we weren't to blame.

"Anybody got any cards? I play a mean pinochle." The china dog inspected his paws lazily.

"Shhh!" the pepper shaker hissed. "We're waiting for Harold."

"Sure, right, I know. But while we wait, maybe some poker?" The china dog raised his eyebrows at us all. I didn't even know he had eyebrows.

Fred was the one to finally crack under the pressure. "Are you awake? Anyone in there?" She thumped the salt shaker on the head with Mr. Boots's parasol. The salt shaker didn't move. "It's not working."

Ty grinned at me. "See? I told you. I knew it wasn't our fault."

Way to revise history, buddy. But I couldn't help grinning back. This was the best news I'd had all week.

"So he's not going to wake up?" The pepper shaker's chin started to wobble.

I got my grin under control and tried to look sympathetic. "I don't think so. I'm sorry."

"Oh." The wobble turned into a lip quiver, and

suddenly pepper was streaming out of the shaker's nose as the shaker sobbed.

I looked helplessly at Ty. I don't know the protocol for comforting sad pepper shakers. Pat on the back? A hug? I didn't want to do the wrong thing. As it turned out, I didn't have to do anything.

"Here, Eunice. Use my sleeve." The salt shaker waddled over and held out his arm.

"Harold!" the pepper shaker squealed.

It was a joyful reunion, okay? Happy times, lots of hugging and squealing and dancing around. And I wanted to be happy for them. Really. But that happy reunion just meant one thing to me.

Ty leaned back, thumping his head against the wall. "Crap, Arlie. It's us."

CHAPTER 5

HERE'S A QUESTION YOU DON'T USUALLY HAVE to answer the second week of school: Who do you get to babysit your newly animated knick-knacks? Strangely enough, there isn't a listing for knickknack babysitters in the yellow pages. Believe me, I checked.

"Oh, don't mind us. Just go to school. We'll be fine and dandy." Fred batted her eyelashes innocently.

Somehow that didn't make me feel better. But we're talking the second week of school here—it's not like we could cut or anything.

And we were going to be pretty close to late as it was.

"Maybe we should bring them with us?" I said doubtfully. But even as I said it, I knew that wasn't going to happen. That china dog had a mouth on it—there was no way I was going to risk it backtalking during science class. And I didn't even want to think about what would happen if Fred got her paws on the clothes in the girls' locker room.

"Those things aren't getting near my backpack," Ty said, which pretty much ended the discussion.

I gave Fred what I hoped was a sufficiently serious look. "You promise to stay in my room? No visits to the kitchen? No exploring?"

The knickknacks exchanged a quick conspiratorial glance and then nodded obediently.

"Sure, no problem. What's to explore, anyway?" The china dog shrugged at me and rolled his eyes. "I've seen the house, kiddo. It's not that great."

I wasn't convinced, but Ty was already putting his backpack on.

"It's the second week of school, Arlie. We have to be there."

I was pretty sure I was going to regret this. And soon. But I totally caved. "All right. Stay here. But you leave this room and get caught, don't come crying to me."

Eunice the pepper shaker nodded, spewing a fresh puff of pepper, and held hooves with Harold. They were cute, but in a make-me-barf kind of way. I didn't trust them for one second."Fred, you're in charge of the dragonfly while I'm gone."

"Gotcha." Fred smirked as she reclaimed the pendant and tucked it discreetly under her bonnet.

That would have to be good enough. I ran through the house quickly before we left to try to find Mom's Egyptian cat statue, but he was making himself scarce. I crossed my fingers that he would stay hidden until I got back. We were about two seconds away from missing the first bell, so I zipped up my fifty-ton backpack and we booked it to school as fast as we could.

Even at a half trot, it was hard not to notice some changes around town. Let me put it this way—it's not every day that a flock of pink plastic lawn flamingos passes you on the street.

"Are those flamingos doing what I think they're doing?" I really hoped I was imagining things.

"If you're thinking the electric slide, then yes, they are," Ty said through gritted teeth. He's never been a big fan of line dancing.

"Oh, that is not good," I breathed as the flamingo flock disappeared into the trees behind Amber Vanderklander's house.

"Tell me about it."

Pink plastic lawn flamingos are pretty noticeable, even when they're not doing choreographed disco moves. If they weren't on the front page of the paper yet, it was only a matter of time.

"Had to touch them all, didn't you? Good going, Ty."

Ty shot me a nasty look. "Nobody will notice, okay? Who notices flamingos, anyway?"

I just hoped he was right.

When we got to school, though, it was pretty obvious everybody in town had noticed at least one of the disappearances.

"Hey, did you guys hear about the Happy Hog?" Marty Bollinger sprayed me with his potato chip breakfast as we hustled up the front walk. He's never been good at the closing-your-mouth-while-you're-chewing thing. "It's totally gone! Amber thinks the seniors from Courtland High kidnapped it."

I nodded and flicked potato chip slime off of my collar. "That's probably it. They're trying to psych us out."

"Well it won't work! We'll pound them!" Marty gurgled as the bell rang. He licked his greasy fingers and ducked into the school.

I shot Ty a look. "If they think it was kidnapped, that's a good thing, right?"

Ty nodded. "Right. They won't suspect it's come to life. Not until it storms the school and eats all the kids for lunch." He gave me a grim smile. That's the best thing about Ty. He's always so upbeat.

I gave a choked laugh. "Yeah, really funny." I felt cold inside, though. After all those years of abuse outside the Happy Mart, it wouldn't surprise me if that Hog had a huge chip on his shoulder. And who knew what a big plastic hog was capable of?

"Meet at the library at study hall?" Ty yelled over his shoulder at me as we rushed in opposite directions to class. I nodded and scooted into Spanish class just as the final bell rang.

That day had to be the slowest moving day ever. And I can't even begin to say what a joy it was to spend those superlong minutes with Señora Jenkins. I'm lousy at Spanish on my good days, which this was not, so naturally, Señora Jenkins immediately zeroed in on me. I was her go-to girl for every single question. Thankfully, since she insists on talking only in Spanish, I had no clue what she was snapping at me about. Sometimes ignorance really is bliss.

Part of my problem was what was happening at home, sure, but as soon as I'd opened my backpack, I'd realized I had a bigger problem, code name: Mr. Boots. At some point during the salt shaker vigil Mr. Boots had apparently decided to move from the top of the refrigerator to the bottom of my backpack, which would have been fine, except he'd never left. So when I reached in to take out my Spanish notebook, I got slimed by a set of quivering dog nostrils.

I don't care what anybody says, dogs are kind of frowned upon in school. I had to discreetly drape a Kleenex over his head so I wouldn't blow his cover. And you can't tell me that watching a Kleenex in the depths of your backpack getting sucked in and out isn't distracting. I'm sure there are studies to back me up here.

So it was a huge relief when study hall finally rolled around and I was able to meet Ty in the library.

"Why are you carrying half your books?" Ty looked up from the table in the corner. "Something wrong with your bag?"

I slammed my books down and held out my bag for his inspection. I heard Mr. Boots cussing from somewhere deep inside. "I think he ate my lunch."

Ty shrugged. "He probably had to, to save himself from being crushed. How much junk do you have in there, anyway?"

I gave him a frosty stare. "My book bag is hardly the issue here." I plunked it on the floor by the chair, careful not to dump Mr. Boots out completely. I figured a little jostling wouldn't kill the guy. He was a stowaway, after all. He's lucky I wasn't making him walk the plank.

"Right." Ty put on his serious face. "The dragonfly pendant. Well, what's the plan? As far as I can tell, we're totally screwed." Ty closed his eyes and leaned back in the chair until he was teetering dangerously on two legs. "Am I right?"

I shook my head. "Not if we figure out how it works."

Ty lurched forward, slamming the chair back into place with a loud bang. Mrs. Marshall, the librarian, shot us a warning look. I hoped she wouldn't come over. She douses herself in enough perfume to mask toxic-waste fumes, and my nose just couldn't take it right now. I hadn't even gone near her but I could still smell Heaven's Passion or whatever today's perfume of choice was. She likes to mix it up a little.

Thankfully, Ty must've felt the same way, because he lowered his voice. "We know how it works. We need to know how to make it stop working."

I nodded. "And fast." I tried not to think about what was happening in my room right now. I've seen the show *Trading Spaces* before, and I didn't much like the idea of coming home to a total room makeover. And I wouldn't put it past Fred.

Ty patted a pile of books on the table. "Mrs. Marshall helped me out—these are all about jewelry and local history. I told her it was a class project. I'm figuring that dragonfly pendant has to be in one of them. Something like that had to have made news at some point, right?"

"Right." I grabbed a book. I was willing to try anything at this point.

We jumped right in, but talk about a needle in a haystack. I couldn't even find the haystack. Plus, it didn't help that I could totally tell that Mrs. Marshall had touched all those books. Perfume wafted around the table whenever I turned the page.

Then suddenly, it was like I was in the eye of the perfume hurricane.

"I'm so proud of you two, so studious so early in the year." My nose had fled for cover long before I looked up and saw Mrs. Marshall smiling down at us. I smiled happily and held my breath in what I hoped was a discreet way. I figured if she didn't leave before I passed out, at least I'd be unconscious, right?

Mrs. Marshall patted Ty's shoulder. "Good work, kids. Let me know if you need anything." Ty gave her the thumbs-up but didn't say anything. I think he was holding his breath too. He was going to have to wash that shirt when he got home, that's for sure.

Mrs. Marshall gave him an uncertain thumbs-up back and then headed back across the library. Ty slammed his book shut. "This is ridiculous, Arlie. This is no help at all. The jewelry books don't have anything about our town, and the local history books don't have anything about jewelry. We're never going to find out about that dragonfly pendant."

"What dragonfly pendant?" Christie O'Dell drifted over beside Ty. I don't know how long she'd been hovering nearby, or how much she'd heard. I can tell you, though, if people started finding out about the pendant and what it did, we could pretty much pack it in and hit the road. Heck, Sheriff Shifflett would probably give us a kick start, if you know what I mean.

"Hi, Ty." Christie smiled as she slid into the seat next to him. "What are you guys talking about? What pendant?"

Ty scowled down at the table. "Why does this have to be a stupid junior-senior high? Why can't it just be senior high?" he muttered under his breath. Not that

66

quietly either—I totally think Christie heard him.

"My dad's a jeweler. Did you know that?" If she'd heard him, she didn't act like it. Christie had beams of adoration shooting out of every pore. Ty's whole running-away thing yesterday was starting to make a whole lot of sense.

"Yeah, that's great. I've got a thing to do. You know, at the place. See you." Ty pushed the books away, grabbed his book bag, and disappeared into the library stacks.

Christie didn't even seem that fazed; she just turned and looked at me instead. Talk about an uncomfortable situation. I tried to smile and fiddled with the edge of my shirt. I needed to make my escape, and fast, but I wasn't sure how to do it.

"Arlie? Can I ask you a question?"

Crud. All chances for an easy exit were blown. "Yeah, I guess." I prayed it had nothing to do with the dragonfly.

"And please, you can tell me the truth." Christie fidgeted in her seat and wiped her nose. I sat frozen, staring at her like a smiley lump of lameness.

What did she think I was going to say? Did she seriously expect me to be like, Oh yeah, that pendant? Brings things to life, no big deal. So, nice weather, huh?

Christie looked at me intently. It really gave me the creeps. I wished she would just get it over with.

"Just say it, Christie." I probably sounded a little more hostile than I meant to, but I didn't appreciate her cat-with-a-mouse routine.

"So, you and Ty. Are you a couple?" Christie blinked at me and fiddled with her barrette.

You know how sometimes someone asks you a question that makes your brain completely freeze up, and all you can do is gurgle and try to not to drool down your front? It was like that.

"I can understand if you guys are keeping it secret and all, but I just need to know if you guys are serious. You know, so I can plan my moves." Christie looked at me again, like she honestly expected me to be able to make words and say them. But, really, at this point, speech was not even in the realm of possibility.

Christie shifted in her seat and waited. I had to try to say something.

"I. Uh. Me and Ty . . ." It came out like more of a weird half snort. It was like I was trying to speak a foreign language or something (and, as Señora Jenkins will tell you, I sure as heck can't do that). But Christie seemed to get the message. What message she got, I have no idea.

"Thanks, Arlie. I get it. Thanks for being straight with me." She blushed and zipped away from the table before I had a chance to figure out what had just happened. Ty peeked around the bookshelf behind me.

"Did she leave? What did she want?" Ty hissed at me, pretending to be reading a book about petroleum engineering.

"She . . ." I didn't even know how to explain it. "I think she likes you."

"Well, duh. Is she gone?" Ty peered around nervously.

"Yeah. I think so." I half stood up to get a better view of the door, and boy did I wish I hadn't. Because as Christie walked out, Bethany Burgess and Tina walked in. And they were headed straight for me.

"Well well well, look who's here, Tina." Bethany had honed in on me like a duck on a junebug, and she wasn't afraid to use her outdoor voice to make her disgust known. Everyone in the room instantly picked up on it, and turned their receptors to the Bethany channel. Even Mrs. Marshall's ears were perked, and she was straining to hear every word. She wasn't fooling anybody with that whole "I'm just putting books on a cart" act.

I took a deep breath and braced myself to face Bethany. I had this whole speech I'd worked out for when I saw her. It was awesome, if I do say so myself. Part of it even rhymed. But face-to-face, her incredible Bethany powers of coolness rendered me helpless. And the fact that Tina was there as backup only made things worse.

"Bethany, uh, hi. Look, I . . . um . . ." I stopped and

started again. And I mean literally. Even the "Bethany, uh, hi" part. It was mortifying.

"Yeah?" Bethany tossed her hair at me in a threatening, Charlie's Angels about-to-kick-butt kind of way.

I opened my mouth and tried to force even a part of my awesome speech out.

"Look, sorry, okay?" I said it all in one huge rush.

Voilà—apology mission completed. That was good enough, right?

Tina blinked at me. "What, that's it?"

Yeah, I knew it wasn't what Mom had in mind. But it's what I was going with. I'd had a rough day. And it was starting to hit me what a horrible mistake it probably had been to leave those crazed knickknacks alone in my room. Bethany was the least of my problems.

Bethany and Tina crossed their arms and got into a fighting stance. It looked good—they were in sync and everything. I had to move fast.

"Ty, I'm sick, okay? I'm going home. Now." I picked up my book bag, totally forgetting that Mr. Boots was using it as his personal trailer. He was half out when I scooped it up and ended up dangling from the strap by one foot. I grabbed him by the collar of his hoodie sweatshirt and stuffed him back inside. I like to think that nobody noticed.

"That's IT?" Tina was just getting started, I could tell. She'd be in full-rage mode in five minutes.

"She thinks that'll make it okay? What's wrong with her?" Bethany looked seriously shocked. She whacked Tina on the arm. "Your sister's mental, Tina."

I didn't wait for the fireworks. I just pushed my way past them, walked out of the library, down the hall, and all the way out of the school. And once I hit the sidewalk I just kept walking. I didn't even look back once.

I knew I was going to have to pay for cutting class later, but I just had to get home. I don't know what had made me think high school was going to rock. It totally sucked.

I'd worked myself into a pretty good funk by the time I got to my street, and I was planning to head for my room, kick out anything that didn't have a pulse, and hit the cookies hard. But halfway down the street I snapped right out of it.

It's pretty hard to wallow in depression in the middle of a party. And one look at my house with its wide-open door, blaring music, and rowdy plastic squirrels on the stoop told me that my house had turned into party central.

CHAPTER 6

THE PLASTIC SQUIRRELS ON THE FRONT STOOP started giggling like they were half insane when they saw me. I pushed my way past them and ran into the living room, ignoring their angry squeals of protest.

Fred, the shaker twins, and the china dog were in front of the TV, blasting the opening of the movie *Xanadu*. Obviously they'd been in Tina's room and found her stash of 80s DVDs.

"Look, there she is! Check this out, it's just like us!" Fred hopped over to me. She was wearing an off-the-shoulder peasant blouse from Mr. Boots's village-wench period and had some kind of homemade leg warmers on her legs.

They all pointed and cheered ecstatically at the opening of the film. The squirrels must've heard them, because they rushed in from outside, joined hands, and started twirling around the living room.

"Listen, hear that song? They're saying 'I'm alive!' Get it? Get it?" Fred shouted over the squealing squirrels.

I crossed my arms and did my best Mom impression. "I'm familiar with the song." On screen, Olivia Newton-John and her muse sisters popped out of a mural one by one.

"It's just like us, right? They're alive, we're alive, it's our theme song!" Eunice did what I can only assume were some sheep square-dancing moves around the leg of the coffee table. "Check this out. Hit it, guys!"

Instantly Fred, Eunice, the squirrels, and a bunch of other lawn ornaments started doing an elaborate choreographed dance number in front of the TV. It boggled the mind. There were lots of dramatic kicks and arm waving.

And they were totally in sync with the dancers on TV.

I have to admit, I was impressed. But I didn't know what time Mom would be coming home, and I couldn't take any chances, so I reached over and clicked the TV off. Loud groans echoed throughout the room as the music stopped, not just from the dancers, either. I glanced around nervously. Just how many things were in here, anyway?

"What the heck is going on here? You were going to stay in my room!"

"What? You never said we couldn't have friends over." Fred put her hands on her hips.

"Why would I say that? I didn't know you had any friends!"

Fred looked hurt. "Oh, I see. Nobody would want to be friends with me, is that it?"

Good thing I hadn't been planning on a future career as a knickknack diplomat, because my skills were totally lacking. "That's not what I meant! When did you have time to make any friends?"

"No, I get it." Fred sniffed and pulled up her leg warmers. They looked suspiciously like the cuffs on Tina's favorite glitter shirt, but I didn't say anything. What I didn't know wouldn't hurt me, right?

"You don't want me to have any fun. I see how it is." Fred flopped down on the floor and adjusted the bandanna on her head.

I'm pretty sure I would've come up with a snappy comeback, but I was distracted by a loud *thunk* behind me. Mr. Boots had apparently emerged from my book bag long enough to take in the dance number, and was now passed out cold on the linoleum. I didn't blame him. It kind of blew the mind.

"Oh, great. Mr. Boots?" I went over and shook him, but it was no use. Luckily, thanks to Mom's past canine nudity issues we had some smelling salts in the kitchen (or, as Mom insists on calling them, some "aromatherapy crystals"), so I made a quick dash to the kitchen to save the day.

The kitchen stopped me dead, though. Two pink

flamingos were rooting around in the pantry, and the plastic garden penguin that had bruised my hand was lying on his back squirting spray whipped cream into his mouth. From the mess on his face, it looked like he'd been at it for a while. Not cool, in my opinion. And I hate to say it, but there was a lot of pepper on the floor. I mean, a lot of pepper. A whole pile. To be honest, it looked like a housebreaking issue.

"Eunice? Can I ask you a question?" I called into the living room.

I heard hooves trotting across the floor and then Eunice stuck her head in the doorway. "Yes?"

I pointed at the pile. "Did you have an accident?" I was trying to be polite. I don't know what you call it when a shaker dumps pepper.

Eunice blushed. "Not like that! I just, I think I have allergies. Harold suggested it."

Harold appeared next to Eunice. "She's had a runny nose all morning, so I thought she should go on a cleansing diet to clear her system."

"A cleansing diet." Which, for pepper shakers means just unstoppering in the middle of the floor, I guess. "Got it."

Eunice gave me an apologetic smile. "I refilled, though!" She opened her mouth, giving me a glimpse of something white and puffy and vaguely disturbing. I didn't even want to know what I was looking at. But Eunice told me, anyway.

"Mini-marshmallows! I'm feeling much better now. Although I am worried about all that sugar."

"Right." I nodded. This was going to take a lot of getting used to. I made a mental note to process it all later—if I tried to do it now, I was pretty sure my head would explode.

I shooed the flamingos out of the room, took the whipped cream away from the penguin, and threw it in the trash. Nobody was going to want something that had had penguin lips wrapped around it for so long.

I headed back to Mr. Boots, smelling salts at the ready. Something skittered away from him as I walked up, but before I figured out what it was, I noticed Mr. Boots was sitting up and looking around woozily.

I crouched down and wiped the drool from his hoodie, but he didn't seem to notice me at all. It was like he was mesmerized by something behind me in the dining room.

I waved my hand in front of his face.

"Yo, Boots. Hello?" He didn't even react, he just kept staring, and the expression on his face looked like he'd just woken up in Kibble Heaven.

Finally, I couldn't take it anymore. I peered over my shoulder.

Creeping up quietly behind me was the one thing I'd totally forgotten that I'd touched with the dragonfly. Mr. Boots's squeaky bunny.

I was immediately on guard. The last thing I wanted to witness right now was some kind of squeaky revenge and the ensuing carnage. And, to be honest, I wasn't really sure what kind of relationship Mr. Boots had with his squeaky toys. I prepared to grab either the Squeak or Mr. Boots at the first sign of violence. But when the bunny got to Mr. Boots, it nuzzled right up to him, like it was going in for a squeaky toy version of a hug. It even made that squeaky noise that's so pleasant at four in the morning.

For his part, Mr. Boots looked like he'd won the lottery. He jumped to his feet and immediately began prancing around the Squeak, who squeaked back at him and then raced under the dining room table playfully. Mr. Boots dashed after it. I fell backward onto my butt. I don't know why I'd been worried. It was love at first sight.

My relief lasted about two seconds, though, because that's how long it was before an enormous splash in the living room got me on my feet and running. Apparently even Egyptian stone cats have a thing for angel fish. I fished the cat out of the tank, who promptly showed his appreciation by hissing and streaking out of the room, knocking over a small end table in the process.

I'd never realized how rowdy a gang of lawn

ornaments could get before that day. And boy had they done a number on our house. If I was going to keep this a secret, I had my work cut out for me.

I went out onto the stoop, shooed all the remaining squirrels, flamingos, and basically anything that moved inside, and locked the door with the dead bolt. Then I called the school office with my best sick impression to get them to ask Ty to bring me my homework. I'm sorry, but I needed help and lots of it, and there was no way Ty was getting out of this scot-free.

Then I pulled out our *Rudolph the Red-Nosed Reindeer* DVD and hoped it would keep the plastic set entertained. Thankfully I hit the jackpot—they all seemed to identify with the Island of Misfit Toys a little too much. I was psyched they were so into it, but as I came to discover, there are only so many times you can listen to the train whine about the square wheels on his caboose before you want to smack him and hand him an electric sander. So by the time Ty showed up, I'd let them start watching *Xanadu* again, and you know what that does to them. They were choreographing the clothing store dance number when Ty walked in the room. I think he was a little shocked.

"Look, we're watching documentaries!" Fred shrieked when he came in. The excitement was really getting to them.

Ty just nodded and smacked me with a newspaper as he flopped onto the couch. "Check it out. *Daily Squealer,* special edition."

One look at the headline was all I needed to see. I mean, how many things could they mean with the huge quarter-page headline THEY'RE ALIVE.

"So it's out, huh? Everybody knows?" I slumped back into the squishy center of the couch.

"Oh, yeah." Ty nodded. He dug around in his book bag and pulled out another paper, this time the *Daily News.* "But don't worry—it hasn't hit the legitimate papers yet."

I pressed my hands against my eyes. "I don't even want to see it!"

"It's not that bad. Read it—it's about the Happy Hog. Marty was right: They think it was a robbery. According to the *Daily News*, the cops think there's this gang of lawn ornament thieves, maybe doing it as a prank. We're fine."

I took my hands off my eyes and opened them. Eunice and Harold were perched on the cushion next to me staring at me intently. Eunice had a bubble of marshmallow peeking out of one nostril. They both looked really concerned. It would have been touching if it hadn't been so creepy.

I shook my head. This just didn't make sense. "So nobody's seen anything move? Nobody?" I snorted. I'm sorry, but come on. "Nobody's been terrorized by a flock of flamingos? The Hog hasn't attacked anyone's car?" I didn't see how that could be, considering the day I'd had.

"Well . . ." Ty made a *whoops* face at me. "One lady. You know old Mrs. Grover? Not the pharmacist, but her mother."

"Yeah? Spill it."

"She's saying that she saw the Hog walk away on its own. Apparently it waved to her."

I groaned. "It waved?"

Ty suddenly looked really interested in the carpet. "And there have been a couple of reports that it was seen boozing it up down at Jimmy's Lounge. But nobody believes those."

I blinked. "The Happy Hog was boozing it up down at Jimmy's Lounge? Seriously?"

I pictured the Happy Hog sitting on a barstool, and the sad thing is, it wasn't hard to do. "But Ty, he's got no pants. What about 'no shirt, no shoes, no service'?"

Ty grinned. "I don't hear 'no pants' anywhere in that rule."

"They'd serve a hog with no ID? Really?" Jimmy's Lounge was even sleazier than I'd thought.

Ty shrugged. "The bartender says it isn't true—he says he'd remember serving a giant hog in a chef's hat. He says if it was there, it was only drinking club soda."

"Club soda. Well. That makes it fine, then." I couldn't believe Ty wasn't taking this more seriously.

"Arlie, the point is, nobody believes it. They think it's all made up." Ty slumped back onto the couch. "But we've got to do something. Your parents are totally going to notice the lawn ornament fiesta you've got going on here. You're just lucky Tina hasn't shown up yet. She and Bethany kind of got into it after you left."

I knew he was right. But I didn't have the slightest idea what to do about it. "You think I don't want to? Come on, where am I supposed to hide these guys? They're not exactly easy to overlook." I watched as a couple of plastic bunnies leapfrogged around the living room, wiping out in the middle of the china dog's poker match.

Suddenly Ty sat bolt upright and stared at me with a maniacal gleam in his eye. "I know one place."

I stared at him doubtfully. "Really?" I tried not to get my hopes up. Ty's plans have a pretty high failure rate.

"Arlie, if you were a lawn ornament, where would

you want to hang out? If you could pick just one place, where would you go?" Ty gave me a knowing glance, and waggled his fingers over his head like they were antennae.

I grinned. I couldn't believe I hadn't thought of it before. "Mandy's."

CHAPTER 7

I JUMPED UP AND CLAPPED MY HANDS. "OKAY, everybody! We're going camping! Everybody get ready—we're heading out in five minutes!"

I'd never seen plastic creatures move so fast. They were like tiny speeding missiles of kitsch.

"I need a coat!" Fred shrieked, struggling to hop up the stairs. But she's ten inches tall, tops, so stairs are a challenge.

Eunice tugged on my pants leg. "I'b all stupped ub." Gooey marshmallow bubbles appeared in both nostrils.

Harold gave me an apologetic smile. "Marshmallows probably weren't the best idea."

I sighed. "Go change, we'll wait." I didn't even want to know how Eunice's marshmallow insides had gotten heated up.

Eunice and Harold skittered into the kitchen. I hoped she'd find a more discreet place to unstopper this time. I'd managed to tidy up while they were watching TV, but I had a feeling Mom would notice a pile of marshmallow leavings on the kitchen floor.

At the end of five minutes almost all of them had made it back into the entryway. Most of them didn't look any different, though, so I wasn't sure what all that racing around had been for. Fred came tumbling down the stairs wearing Mr. Boots's green plaid cape and matching cap just as I started the instruction portion of the day.

"Now we're going to a fun camping ground, but first we have to get there without anyone seeing you."

Ty snorted. "Good luck."

I glared at him. "So what we're going to do is be

really quiet, and when I say freeze, everybody freeze. Pretend you can't move. Got it?"

The lawn ornaments looked at each other uncertainly. We were losing them.

"It's a game!" I cheered, high-fiving Ty. (Or I tried to. Ty didn't notice what I was doing in time and I kind of smacked him in the head.)

There was a murmur of understanding and much nodding of heads. I had everyone do a few practice runs and when they seemed to have the hang of it, I grabbed my backpack.

"Eunice! We're leaving!" I called into the kitchen. Harold and Eunice came skittering out, Eunice discreetly wiping her nose with her hoof. I couldn't tell what she'd filled up with, but I had a sinking feeling that I'd be finding out before long. I made a point of putting a few extra Kleenex in my pocket.

I herded Fred, the china dog, and the shaker twins into my backpack, because I'm sorry, Mandy lives pretty far away and I wasn't willing to wait for those guys to walk the equivalent of twenty knickknack miles. I zipped up the backpack, threw open the door, and promptly slammed it again. We had a problem.

"What?" Ty looked at me like I was a crazy person. "Aren't we leaving?"

I twitched the curtain in the window aside and peeked out. "Cookie and Mrs. Big Cookie. Ten o'clock."

Ty peeked out. "You need to learn your clock, Arlie. Try two o'clock."

I ignored him. It was hardly the time to get technical. The point was, we had a Cookie situation on our hands.

Cookie and Mrs. Big Cookie were hanging out in their front yard for no apparent reason (except maybe to torment me). Mrs. Big Cookie was stretched out on one of those foldable lawn recliners, and Cookie was shrieking and throwing her Barbies onto the driveway as hard as she could. What did I tell you? Cute.

"Shoot, Arlie, we don't have time for them." Ty Parker, once again master of the understatement.

I grabbed the cordless and gave Ty a smug smile. "Trust me. Piece of cake." I dialled Mrs. Big Cookie's number and waited for her to jump up and race inside. I figured there's no way she'd miss a phone call. When it went to voice mail, I did it again. And again. Mrs. Big Cookie sipped a glass of lemonade and waggled her flip-flop around. Not the reaction I was hoping for. I'm thinking the woman has hearing issues.

"Piece of cake, huh?" Ty took the cordless out of my hand and hung up. "Face it, Arlie. She's not budging."

I looked at the clock. Mom would be home anytime now. I knew what I had to do.

I swung my backpack back over my shoulder (to a chorus of squeals from inside) and opened the door. "I'll distract her—move out when she's not looking."

Ty nodded. "Got it. Good luck."

We did a fist-bump and then I marched over to Mrs. Big Cookie's house.

Mrs. Big Cookie looked up as I walked over, and I have to say, the expression on her face didn't warm my heart. She looked like she'd suddenly discovered her house was infested with huge annoying vermin, and guess who was playing the role of the vermin? You got it. Me. She put on a big fakey smile, though, and tried to be welcoming, so I have to give her points for that.

"Arlene, hello. What brings you here?" Mrs. Big Cookie caught a rebounding Barbie head and handed it back to Cookie, who stuck her tongue out and pointedly ignored me. It was a snub, but I was fine with it. Attention from Cookie is the last thing I need.

I took a deep breath. "I wanted to apologize for yesterday. I shouldn't have screamed. And snatched Fred. And run away."

Mrs. Big Cookie nodded and squinted up at me.

"Thank you, Arlene. That's nice of you. But you know you completely traumatized Cookie. I'm just hoping she doesn't need therapy."

It seemed to me that Cookie definitely needed some pretty serious therapy, because she was one warped kid. But I didn't think Mrs. Big Cookie would appreciate my input there. So I just nodded and made my sad puppy face.

She pointed to Cookie sadly. "See? She's still not back to her old self."

I'd positioned myself so that Mrs. Big Cookie would have to look away from my house to see me. She had no idea that Ty and a stream of lawn ornaments were sneaking slowly out of my front door. It was some clever maneuvering on my part, but I hadn't figured on Cookie's powers of observation.

Cookie had decapitated all of her Barbies and was standing stock-still, staring across the street. She'd totally forgotten about the Barbie arm she was in the process of ripping off and was gaping at the plastic creatures creeping down the street.

I tried not to look, but it was difficult, because they weren't exactly being discreet the way I'd hoped. Especially that troublemaking garden penguin—turning and waggling your butt at a six-year-old is a pretty obvious statement.

"MOM!" Cookie shrieked, pointing at the penguin-butt action. She must've gotten into some kind of pointing-and-shrieking groove, because it didn't seem like she had any intention of stopping.

My heart practically stopped. But thankfully, Ty must've given the signal, because all of the lawn ornaments across the street instantly froze. Ty leaned against a tree and tried to whistle nonchalantly.

Mrs. Big Cookie jumped up and rushed to Cookie. I didn't blame her for being concerned—I was afraid Cookie's lungs were going to pop out of her mouth with one of those screams.

"Thank you for the apology, Arlene, but we'll go inside now." She glanced across the street at the lawn ornaments and made some kind of retchy noise in the back of her throat.

"Excuse me?" I was hoping the noise wasn't directed at me. It was pretty gross for an adult noise.

Mrs. Big Cookie shook her head like I was a buzzy little gnat. "Not you, just the junk people insist on putting on their lawns. It's disgusting, if you ask me. But never mind. Now that I'm with the homeowners association, we'll get rid of all that."

I scanned the street. "Junk?" I had a feeling she was insulting my plastic buddies. Somebody in my backpack did too, because I heard a little huffy snort.

She nodded at the garden penguin across the street, caught mid butt waggle. "That plastic trash. It's just an eyesore. It has no place in a decent neighborhood, if you ask me. But thanks again for stopping by, Arlene."

She picked up Cookie, who should've had the decency to pass out by now from all that screaming, and hustled inside.

I waited until I was sure they were gone before I gave Ty the signal and we took off running toward Mandy's house. I could hear some muffled ranting coming from inside my book bag, but I wasn't about to stop and find out what was going on in there.

It was like a weird game of red light–green light getting to Mandy's house—we'd all run at top speed until we got to the corner, everybody would freeze while we checked to make sure it was clear, and then we'd take off again.

I'm really shocked that we didn't get busted. Or, at least, nobody said anything. If anyone saw us, I have a feeling they chalked it up to a bad reaction to medication and went inside to lie down. And once we'd made it to Mandy's, we were home free.

Mandy Burke is this homeschooler girl me and Ty met over the summer, and she lives in this pink-frosted-cupcake-type house with a yard filled to the brim with all kinds of tinkly fairies, gnomes, and lawn ornaments—seriously, if you can imagine it, it's at Mandy's house. So naturally our lawn guys thought they'd gone to heaven. The only problem was that this version of heaven was creepy and inanimate.

"Why aren't they moving?" A squirrel sidled up to me nervously as I unzipped my backpack.

"They're sleeping," I lied. I don't know how to talk to squirrels. Especially plastic ones.

The squirrel thumped a plastic skunk on the tail. "His eyes are open. Who sleeps with their eyes open?" he said doubtfully.

"That guy does," I said. I didn't have time for explanations, as if I had any. Right now, I had to find Mandy.

"Did you hear what she SAID?" Fred yelled as she climbed out of my backpack. "Trash? Who is she, anyway?"

"Don't you remember Cookie?" I said, motioning toward Fred's head.

"You mean . . . YOU DON'T MEAN . . ." Fred looked appalled.

"I do." Yeah, I know I probably shouldn't say anything, but I figured Fred had a right to know.

Fred's eyes widened and she stared at me in horror as I headed around the house to find Mandy. Ty was way ahead of me, though. He stopped me with an agonized look. "Safari," he hissed at me, took a deep breath, and turned the corner.

I peeked around after him. It wasn't hard to see what

he meant. Mandy is a couple of years older than us, but she acts younger, what with her costumes and portraits and stuff. Me and Ty have been her unfortunate victims more than once. (Ask Ty about his deelybopper portrait sometime—trust me, he loves that.) Today she was all decked out like a big-game hunter, with a pith helmet and khaki outfit. I could see a fake-fur lion's mane on the table next to her. I made a silent vow right then—no matter what happened, I was not putting that thing on.

But thankfully, even though she was all decked out for a safari, Mandy didn't seem to be in the costume mode. It actually looked like she was just studying. It was weird.

"Oh, hi guys!" She waved when she saw us and held up a textbook. "Science time."

"Oh sure, okay." Apparently homeschooling isn't all paintings and party time. I was kind of bummed. It was like finding out the Tooth Fairy takes a course load of dental hygiene classes on the side. "Not safari time?"

Mandy's face lit up. "If you can wait half an hour. It'll be awesome! I've got my paints all ready. And Puffkins is inside getting into character."

Puffkins is Mandy's cat, and he's featured in pretty much all of her paintings. He's not a happy cat, to put it mildly.

Ty shook his head. "Sorry. We just wanted to ask a quick favor."

Mandy cocked her head. "What is it?"

I smiled. "Not much. We just had some lawn ornaments that I didn't want my mom to see."

"They're a present," Ty lied.

I glared at him. I didn't love the idea of lying to Mandy, especially since I didn't think we needed to. "Not a present. I just don't want her to see them. Can I keep them here for a little while?"

Mandy shrugged. "Sure, no problem. Sheesh, you made it sound like a big deal!" She laughed, and then picked up the lion mane. "Are you sure you can't stick around? This would look great on you!"

I shook my head. "Sorry. Maybe later, though. Good luck with the science!"

"Oh, okay." Mandy looked gloomy. I felt like a jerk. It was kind of lousy of us, showing up, ditching our crazed lawn ornaments, and then splitting. That didn't mean I wasn't going to do it; I just felt bad.

We left Mandy to her book and headed back to the lawn ornaments. Thankfully they all seemed to be making themselves right at home. Fred and a bunch of them were all gathered under one of the trees, like they were in a football huddle, or they were plotting something. The only ones who looked uncomfortable were Eunice and Harold.

I pulled Fred aside. "Fred, we're leaving until tomorrow. Can I have the dragonfly back?"

Fred put her paws over her head. "No way, José."

I tried to laugh. "Yeah, funny. Give it back."

Fred shook her head but didn't move her paws. "It's safe with me. Where do you think you'll put it, anyway?"

She had a point, but I didn't want to admit it.

"Are you just leaving us here?" Eunice looked nervous.

"You'll be fine," Ty said. "Mandy said it's okay."

"But we're not outdoor things. We're indoor things." Eunice started to sniffle. Something orange and powdery started coming out of one nostril. I looked away. I so didn't want to know.

"You'll be okay, Eunice, I promise. Now, Fred?" I was losing patience.

"No dice, chickie. Trust me. It'll be fine. What am I going to do?" Fred grinned at me. I didn't trust that kangaroo as far as I could throw her (and that was pretty far, actually).

I looked at Ty for support, but he just shrugged. Even Eunice and Harold had turned and wandered off.

I gave up. "Fine. But leave it in the head. And don't call attention to yourself. You all need to be discreet." Famous last words, right? But what could I do?

Fred bounced happily and adjusted her cap. "I'm the keeper! It's mine mine mine!"

Yeah, that made me feel warm and fuzzy inside. But I gathered up my backpack and headed down the street without a backward glance. As far as I could tell, it was a lose-lose situation.

Ty caught up after a couple of steps. "Look on the bright side, Arlie," he said, thumping me on the back. "Chances are it'll wear off overnight. I bet tomorrow they'll be just regular lawn ornaments again."

"I hope you're right, Ty. I really hope you're right."

CHAPTER 8

I'LL ADMIT IT. PART OF ME WANTED TO GO HOME and never go back to Mandy's again. Just make it all her problem. Sure, I probably wouldn't have done it. But we'll never know, because as soon as I opened my book bag, the ditch-and-run option flew out of the window.

"We're not outdoor things," Harold said apologetically. "And I think Eunice needs a change."

Eunice shrugged, and bright orange puffs came out of her nostrils. Her face had a slightly jaundiced look. She pointed at her nose. "Tang," she explained.

"I think it was a bad idea." Harold shook his head.

"I like it—I feel like a dragon!" Eunice giggled at Harold. "Or an astronaut!"

Ha-ha. Real funny. "You guys were supposed to stay at Mandy's!" I wailed. Now that my book bag had apparently become the most popular form of public transportation, I was going to have to watch it like a hawk.

"He didn't go, why should we?" Eunice pointed at the floor of my room, where Mr. Boots and Squeak were frolicking around like they were on an animated greeting card.

"Well, yeah, but . . ." I didn't know how to explain to Eunice that there was no way I was getting between Mr. Boots and his soul mate. Besides, Squeak wasn't that noticeable, right?

I tried the tough-love route. "Tomorrow morning before school, you're going back. Got it?"

Eunice's chin quivered. I knew I was being manipulated, but Eunice was a master. "And then you'll come pick us up tomorrow night?" Eunice sniffled. "I can't sleep out there!"

I sighed. Trust me to get the phobic pepper shaker. "Whatever, sure." Call me ol' softie, because I totally caved.

I dug around in my closet and pulled out my old dollhouse, and Eunice and Harold set up housekeeping there. I could hear them rearranging the furniture as I did my homework. And believe me, it's hard to concentrate on math when you can hear a couple of shakers arguing about which side of the room the sofa should go on. I'm only glad they'd settled down by the time Mom came in for her talk.

I'd managed to avoid her for most of the night, and she hadn't seemed to have mentioned things to Dad, so I wasn't that surprised when she knocked on the door for a private chat.

"Arlie, did you apologize to everyone yesterday?" Mom poked her head in the door.

I nodded. "Everyone." Thank goodness we'd run into Mrs. Big Cookie.

Mom smiled approvingly. "See? Now don't you feel better?"

I could hear Squeak under the bed talking to Mr. Boots. I hoped that Mom didn't notice anything unusual.

"Bethany didn't seem to accept the apology so much," I said. "I think she's still mad." I didn't mention that it might be because my apology was so lame.

Mom frowned. "Hmm. Well, maybe you need to go out of your way with her. We'll think of something special you can do."

Suddenly I had a brain wave. It was such a crazy idea that it would either be perfect or an incredibly stupid move. So naturally, I was itching to try it.

"How about I invite Bethany to dinner tomorrow?

Along with Tina's boyfriend, Deputy Ben? Wouldn't that be a fun apology? Plus, it's a nice surprise for Tina."

Okay, I know—Tina's boyfriend's a deputy sheriff, and inviting the cops and my archnemesis into a house infested with living knickknacks seems majorly dumb, right? Except at dinner, Bethany would distract Tina, maybe by pounding me a little bit, and in the meantime, I could find out what the cops knew about the whole knickknack situation. I figured it was worth a try.

Mom looked really touched. "That's so sweet! Good idea, Arlie. You can ask Bethany at school, and I'll call Ben in the morning. Don't study too late, now." She blew me a kiss and closed the door quietly.

Eunice stuck her head out of the dollhouse window. "You really need to clean in here more. And do you think I'm getting clumpy?" Eunice did a little hip-swiveling action. I could hear her insides swishing around, and yeah, to be honest, she sounded a little clumpy. But there was no way I was going downstairs to find a Tang substitute.

"Sounds fine," I lied. My plan had better work.

I was not pleased about having to wake up early enough to hike all the way out to Mandy's first thing in the morning, but it's a good thing I did.

Because guess what, they didn't change back overnight. And it was bad. I almost dropped my backpack when I got to Mandy's. Eunice and Harold screamed, that's how big the jolt was.

I had turned the corner and was hiking up the street to Mandy's house when a baseball bounced in front of me and a horde of lawn chipmunks, squirrels, and a bumblebee raced after it.

"What the heck is this?" I bellowed. Yeah, I know it was like seven in the morning, but I was ticked.

The troupe of ornaments stared at me like I'd just hopped off the crazy train and started whispering amongst themselves. Fred bounced up behind them and pushed through the crowd.

"What's the problem, Arlie? It's morning, okay? Keep it down."

"Keep it down? Me, keep it down? What are you guys doing?" I was shaking, I was so mad.

Fred rolled her eyes at me. "It's a little thing called baseball, Arlie? Look it up."

"This is being discreet? You're supposed to stay hidden." This was not good. I just hoped the paper boy hadn't been by yet, but I had a bad feeling he had been, considering there was a whole pile of newspapers just lying on the side of the road. I tried to convince myself it was just take-a-free-paper day and put it out of my mind.

A lawn bumblebee and a happy plastic frog edged up next to me and picked up the baseball carefully, like they were afraid I'd turn on them at any second. I pointed at them accusingly. "And who are these guys? I don't remember any frogs or bumblebees before."

The frog and bumblebee both froze, like if they

didn't move, I wouldn't see them. Suddenly a thought so horrible hit me that I gasped out loud. The frog and bumblebee both jumped back an inch, and then turned and ran for their lives. "Fred, tell me you didn't."

Fred inspected her paw like she was incredibly bored. "Didn't what?"

"Did you make new ones? Have you been using the dragonfly?"

Fred glared at me. "We needed two teams, Arlie. For baseball? How are we supposed to have enough players otherwise? Besides, those frozen guys were just too creepy."

I gasped again. I couldn't believe that kangaroo.

One of the stone lions from in front of the town library wandered out from behind Mandy's house and yawned.

Fred pretended it wasn't there.

"The library lions? You used it on the library lions? How could you do that?" My mind was reeling. "Did you go into town?"

Fred shrugged. "Just me and one of the flamingos. We needed outfielders!"

I closed my eyes and tried to think happy thoughts. But unfortunately the thoughts that kept popping up were of pinking shears, murder, kangarooburgers. I should've let Cookie do her worst.

"Could we get out now please?" A muffled Harold called from inside my backpack.

I'd totally forgotten about Eunice and Harold, but I didn't care. I crouched down to Fred's level and looked her straight in the eye. "You do not make new ones, okay Fred? I don't care what you need them for."

"Okay, fine. It's not like you said not to use the dragonfly. Whatever." Fred pouted.

"It's a little warm, please. Feel free to unzip any-time." Harold's voice was sounding a little hysterical. I hoped I wouldn't have to add claustrophobia to their list of issues.

I unzipped my backpack and tried to figure out what to do about Fred as the shaker twins crawled out. She totally didn't get it. Somebody was going to notice those lions were missing, and thanks to a little thing called homeroom, I couldn't do a thing about it. "I'll be back in a few hours, and when I get here, I don't want to find a baseball game, okay? Keep quiet and keep out of sight. Especially the lions."

Fred hardly even seemed to be paying attention.

"Make it a game!" I said desperately. "See who can find the best hiding place."

"Yeah, sounds real fun." Fred grabbed Eunice and Harold by the hooves. "Come on, guys. You play any sports?"

I had a sudden impulse to lunge out and grab Fred, maybe shake her upside down until the dragonfly fell out of her head. I knew she wouldn't like it, but I figured it wouldn't hurt her. Luckily, I restrained myself in time. I didn't think the lawn ornaments would take too kindly to that, and there were an awful lot of them. And those library lions had mouths as big as my head.

I headed off to school, hoping Ty might have some

idea what to do about the lawn guys. They were completely out of control. But when I found Ty, he had turned into Mr. Goodtimes Happypants overnight.

"Hey Arlie, guess what I heard? Guess!" He tried to give me a high-five, but I left him hanging. I was not in the mood. Ty didn't even seem to care though.

"The thieves have struck again, and guess what they've taken this time? Guess!" He nudged me in the ribs. "I'll give you a hint—it's good news for us, because it has absolutely nothing to do with either you or me." He chuckled happily and did a little end-zone type dance.

"Are we talking . . . oh, I don't know, library lions here?"

Ty stopped dancing and looked disappointed. "Oh, you heard already?"

"Yeah, you could say that." So sue me, I was in a crabby mood-spoiling mood.

"Did Marty tell you? He's really into this story.

Doesn't matter, though, because that is p-r-o-o-f that we didn't do it." He spelled it out and everything.

"Yeah, I heard it from a little orange kangaroo with no brain. Apparently lions make great outfielders."

I'd expected a reaction from Ty, but not the reaction that I got. He turned three shades paler than usual and swayed a little on his feet. I seriously thought he was going to pass out.

"Don't freak out, okay? I told Fred to keep them hidden. But we've got to come up with a plan."

Ty shook his head. "I'm guessing you didn't hear that whole story then? About the lions?"

My stomach lurched like I was on a roller coaster. I really hoped I wasn't about to throw up—that would kill my reputation faster than anything Bethany could do. "What's the rest of it?"

Ty looked miserable. "You know that lady with the chickens who lives on Butler Street? Well, she's not exactly the lady with chickens anymore, if you know what I mean. She says she saw the lions in her yard having lunch—that's how the cops noticed they weren't at the library."

I sat down on the floor. I didn't care that I was right in the middle of the hallway, people would just have to walk around me. Ty sat next to me. "I didn't think they'd do that kind of thing." I was really glad I hadn't shaken the dragonfly out of Fred's head earlier. I could've ended up an in-between-meal snack faster than you can say lion kibble.

Ty shrugged apologetically. "It makes sense, though. They're lions."

I suddenly had a bad feeling about the real reason those lions agreed to be outfielders. I really didn't want to go back to Mandy's and find them all alone in the yard, picking their teeth with flamingo legs.

". . . and so I looked out of the window, and I swear to God it was that Happy Hog? You know the one that's missing? And it looked like it was MOVING." Donna Cavillari's voice drifted over from the other side of the hallway where she was talking to Amber Vanderklander. I nudged Ty guiltily. He just nodded and stared at the floor.

"That is so weird," Amber said. "What did you do?"

"Well, my dog Ted just went insane. You know how he can use the phone? Well, he brought me the cordless. He'd already hit the speed dial for 911. The cops came over, but they didn't find anything, except someone had really messed up the yard, and there were all these empty candy wrappers. Weird, huh? Who would dig up the grass and leave a big patch of dirt?"

I tried not to look at Ty. A big hog definitely seemed to fit the bill there.

"That's super creepy," Amber said, shifting her books. "Hey, Brad. Guess what happened to Donna?"

Donna and Amber had spotted this new senior, Brad Palmer, and hurried after him giggling.

"We need a plan." Ty played with a piece of gross floor fluff.

"Bethany and Deputy Hotstuff are coming to dinner tonight. So I'll get the scoop. Shoot, Bethany!" I jumped up. I still hadn't asked her yet, and if she didn't show, it would ruin the plan. "Mandy's after school?"

Ty grimaced. "Do we have a choice?"

Well, not really, and I wasn't any happier about it than Ty was. I hurried off to find Bethany. If we couldn't stop the dragonfly, at least I could find out how much trouble we were in.

CHAPTER 9

"FIRST THING WE DO IS GET THAT DRAGONFLY back from Fred. No way is she keeping it," I said to Ty as we headed over to Mandy's. Not that getting it back would be easy. Fred wasn't one to give up without a fight, and I wasn't going to be able to take on the whole league of lawn ornaments by myself.

Bethany had agreed to come to dinner, so I had about an hour before I had to head out. I just hoped an hour would be enough.

"I can't believe you actually invited Bethany

over. What, are you feeling suicidal?" Ty snorted.

"Shut up, Ty," I grumbled. Bethany had seemed pretty suspicious and yes, hostile, when I asked her, and I thought for a minute she was going to tell me to stick it. But she'd perked right up when she heard Deputy Hotstuff was going to be there. I figured that was just because that made it seem like more of a party, but I was secretly hoping it meant she'd had a change of heart. Just as long as there weren't any surprises of the inanimate nature, I figured we'd be okay. Plus, Mom was going to make her barbecued cocktail weenies, and who can be grouchy around cocktail weenies?

We got back to Mandy's and thankfully the place was looking pretty quiet compared with that morning. There was general lawn ornament mayhem, sure, but there weren't any obvious sporting matches going on, which I figured was a plus. If you didn't pay too close attention or actually look at any of them, the lawn guys looked like they were just being moved by the breeze. If there was a breeze. And if breezes made you play hopscotch.

Fred was sitting under the tree in a patch of sun. I nodded to Ty. We might as well get this over with.

"Fred, we need that dragonfly," Ty started. "We have to do some research on it." That was the line we'd come up with on the way over. I think it was a pretty good one, if I do say so myself.

Fred smirked at us, took off her hat in a really obvious way, and started fanning herself. "Sorry, guys. No dice."

Fred's head was looking surprisingly intact.

My jaw dropped. "Fred? What happened?"

"Oh, this?" Fred smirked at me. "I had a little work done." She ran a paw over the top of her head.

"Yeah, I can see that." I took a deep breath and asked the big question. "Where's the dragonfly?"

Fred patted herself on the head. "It's safe and sound."

I exchanged a long look with Ty. This was not good. But except for doing my best Cookie impression and excavating the inner workings of Fred's skull, I didn't see what we could do about it. I tried to look on the bright side. Thankfully, Ty did too, and he was more successful than me.

"Well," Ty finally said. "She can't bring anything else to life, right? That's good."

I flopped down onto the grass and leaned my head against the tree. Maybe if I closed my eyes and wished really hard, this would all go away.

Ty sat down next to me. "This buys us a little time, right? So we can figure things out?"

I opened my eyes. Fred waved at me. I never knew that kangaroos were so chipper.

"Not still cranky, are you? About this morning?" Fred scooched closer to me.

I sighed. If I were a lobotomized orange kangaroo who'd just come to life for the first time, I might act the same way Fred was acting. "No," I grumbled.

Ty ignored the touching moment and whipped out a notebook. "As far as I can see, there are three major questions about this thing that we need to answer." He started ticking them off on his fingers. "One—who does it belong to?"

"That's easy. It belongs to me," Fred chipped in.

"No, it doesn't. Cut it out," I said, signaling the end of the touching moment.

Fred stuck her tongue out at me. I hadn't even realized she had a tongue.

Ty ignored us both. "Two—where did it come from?"

"The tree," I said, at the same time Fred piped up with, "Who cares."

Ty gave us both the stink eye. We quieted down.

"And three—how do we find out more about it?" Ty leaned back.

"You forgot number four, how to make things go back." A group of plastic flamingos wandered by, attempting to do a Rockettes-style dance number. I averted my eyes. Nobody should have to see something like that.

"Well, if we can find out more about it, we can figure

that out." Ty rolled his eyes at me like I was braindead.

I picked a piece of grass and inspected it. "I've got an idea about number three." On the walk over, I'd come up with what I figured was a pretty good idea, but it wasn't going to make me win any Ty-sponsored popularity contests.

"Oh, yeah? What are you thinking?"

I didn't look up. I didn't want to see Ty's face. "There's somebody who could maybe help us. Who knows jewelry stuff."

I snuck a quick look at Ty. He was still blissfully unaware.

He nodded. "That sounds good. Who is it?"

I took a deep breath. "Christie O'Dell."

There was nothing but silence. Ty was looking at the ground really hard, and his face was turning all kinds of shades of red. It would've been interesting if I hadn't known he was ready to explode.

"You know. Since her dad's a jeweler?"

Ty still didn't say anything.

Fred looked from me to Ty and back again. "Who's Christie O'Dell?" she said finally.

"Nobody," Ty finally said, jumping to his feet. "That's a stupid idea, and the answer is no."

Seems to me if your dad's a local jeweler, you'll have access to inside information. And it seems to me when your daily life starts including hostile lawn ornaments and flamingo high-kicks, inside information is pretty good to have. Ty was going to have to be flexible on this one. Because if anyone could get information out of Christie O'Dell, he could.

"Just ask her, Ty! If she doesn't know anything, you never have to talk to her again."

Ty was already halfway across the lawn, doing a little half-jump maneuver so he wouldn't squash any of the wandering lawn guys underfoot. Seriously, some of those guys don't seem to understand the rules of self-preservation.

Fred gave a low whistle. A very successful whistle, I might add. How sad is it that a stuffed kangaroo toy is a better whistler than Ty is? I decided to keep that to myself, though. Ty was ticked enough already.

"He's really mad, huh?" Fred whispered.

I nodded and patted Fred on the head. "Your, uh, plastic surgery. How did you do that?"

Fred beamed at me. "Can't even see the stitches, can you? That Mandy's a genius with a needle."

I froze. "You asked Mandy to fix your head?"

Fred shrugged. "She offered, okay?"

Great. I hurried to my feet and ran after Ty, doing a few fancy avoidance jumps of my own. I was going to have to do some fast talking to explain this away. I wouldn't be surprised if Mandy skinned us alive and then posed us as action figures.

When I got around the corner to Mandy's usual place in the backyard, my heart sunk. It was worse than I'd thought. Ty was in a white powdered wig and vest, and he was sitting in an uncomfortable chair. At least, I'm assuming it was uncomfortable, because Ty looked like he'd been stapled into position. Sitting next to him was Mandy's big, white, fluffy cat, Puffkins. Puffkins was dressed as Abraham Lincoln. Puffkins has always been very patriotic.

"Oh hey, Arlie," Mandy said. She had her easel set up across from them and was adjusting the curl on the side of Ty's ear. He shot me a look of desperation, but I pretended I didn't notice. What was I supposed to do?

"I have a bone to pick with you." Mandy whipped out a little comb and brushed Puffkins's beard.

I braced myself for a tirade. I didn't even know what I would say. I mean, how do you apologize for causing a rowdy lawn ornament infestation? "I know, Mandy, and I'm sorry."

Mandy draped the little white ponytail on Ty's wig around his shoulder and adjusted his vest. I have no idea what he was supposed to be. "Yeah, well, you should be. You really need to take better care of your things. Did you see that kangaroo? That hole in its head was huge! I almost couldn't fix it."

I nodded. "It was Cookie, my neighbor. She had

scissors, and I . . . wait, what?" I tried to get a handle on what Mandy was talking about. I didn't actually think the hole in the head was Fred's most noticeable quality right now. I was thinking the breathing, talking thing was a little more noteworthy.

"Yeah, uh, thanks for getting it all fixed up," I finished lamely. I didn't think it was possible that she hadn't noticed Fred and the others were alive, but no way was I mentioning it first.

Ty was mouthing something at me, but I confess, I'm a lousy lip-reader. Honestly, it just looked to me like a giant grouper impression. After a couple of minutes of total incomprehension on my part, he snapped.

"Hey, Mandy," he said, trying to act all cool and nonchalant. "Can you take a Polaroid of me and Puffkins to work from? I think me and Arlie need to go set Cookie straight. She's out of control."

I nodded obediently. I'm no dummy, I can pick up on a new plan in action. "Totally."

Mandy sighed. "I guess, but it won't be the same."

She picked up her digital camera. "Say cheese!"

Poor Ty. You know he's going to feel bad when he and Puffkins are immortalized on Mandy's website. I bit my lip to stop myself from laughing.

"Perfect, thanks," Ty said, trying to look upbeat. I think he did an admirable job. Then he tore the wig and vest off like they were made of 100-percent itch and practically sprinted away. It was tough catching up with him.

"Do you think she knows?" Ty gaped at me. "I don't think she knows!"

"Ty, of course she knows." Really, how could you not know your yard was covered with living lawn ornaments? I mean, they were playing baseball, for goodness' sakes. You can't tell me she didn't know.

"Well, then, she doesn't seem to care." Ty did his freak-out face. I was just glad that Mandy wasn't ready to kill us and evict the lawn guys, because I think we'd have a mutiny on our hands.

"Ty, you can't do surgery on a kangaroo without

noticing that it's moving." Not to mention talking. There's no way Fred could ever shut up for that long.

I felt a tug on my jeans and looked down. Eunice. "You're bringing us back, right? We're ready to go." She clutched my jeans leg with her hooves.

Harold nodded. "We're definitely ready. Please don't leave us alone here again." He leaned closer to me. "Some of these animals . . . they're strange." He widened his eyes significantly, and Eunice twirled a hoof around her head in the universal symbol for crazy.

I sighed. "Sure." I grabbed my backpack and opened it up. "Hop in."

"You guys have all the luck." The china dog groused from underneath a bush. "This place bites."

Eunice hesitated, one leg into the backpack. "You could stay with us. We've got a spare room downstairs."

The china dog's ears perked up. "Really? It's okay?"

Harold and Eunice nodded. The china dog sprang to his feet and scampered over. "You're the best, kiddo." He scurried into the bag and peered up at me from the depths. "Seriously, this place? Out of control."

I nodded. I didn't know what to say.

Turns out, when I got home, my house was just as out of control. Let me put it this way, there was no delicious scent of barbecued cocktail weenies wafting through the air. When I walked through the door, Mom was in the middle of a serious spaz attack.

"Oh, Arlie!" she yelled as I walked though the door. She grabbed me by the shoulders and gave me a tight hug. She squished my backpack and everything. I heard Harold and Eunice clink against each other. (At least I think it was those two. Hard to say for sure, now that the bag was so crowded.)

"Mom?" I tried not to make any sudden movements that might make her freak out more.

"Oh, Arlie, it's terrible!" She looked around nervously, like she expected to be ambushed at any moment. I seriously hoped something hadn't jumped out at her while I was gone. And I'm talking to you, Egyptian stone cat.

"What happened? Are you okay?" I figured I'd take baby steps. You know, get some info before I went into full-confession mode.

Mom grabbed me by the shoulders. "Arlie, we've been robbed."

CHAPTER 10

PRETTY PATHETIC THAT MY FIRST REACTION WAS relief, huh?

"Somebody broke in and robbed us! I called the police and Ben said they're coming. Thank God Tina's got enough sense to date a deputy sheriff!" Mom buried her face in her hands.

Yeah, okay. Thank God. I looked around. The TV was still there, and the stereo was too. Seemed like some pretty crappy burglars to me, but then what do I know? "What did they take?"

Mom sat down on the bench in the entryway and fanned herself. "Little things, mostly, but valuable. It's like they knew exactly what to look for. My antique stone cat statue from Egypt, it's gone. My grandmother's china dog from the mantel—she left that to me in her will! And all of the gnomes out back. I'm not sure what else."

I cleared my throat and put on my most innocent face. "Maybe they're just misplaced? Gnomes don't seem that valuable."

Mom clutched my sleeve. "Arlie, someone came into this house. They went through our things. The gnomes could be to throw us off the track, to make us think it's part of that lawn ornament prank." She pushed her hair back from her forehead. "I didn't even notice at first, can you believe it? Not until I went to get the salt and pepper shakers to put on the table. You know, the ones shaped like little sheep? They're gone too."

I could practically feel the three sets of ears straining from inside my backpack. I just hoped that Mom's stone cat wouldn't decide to make a surprise appearance. I hadn't seen him since he'd tried to eat the angel fish, and honestly? That wasn't a bad thing.

"Maybe Tina took them?" I was desperate here. Seriously, who thought Mom would notice a couple of missing knickknacks?

"That's a very serious accusation, Arlie. Your sister is not a thief." Mom shot daggers at me. Times like this, I could see where Tina got her nasty side from.

"I didn't mean it like that." I stumbled to come up with some kind of plausible explanation. But everything I came up with was too lame to say. I mean, come on, I couldn't really say that she'd brought them to school for a project. Mom wouldn't buy that.

"What did you mean then?" Mom was in full-on frosty mode.

"Maybe a school project?" So sue me, you go with what you have.

"Oh Arlie, that's ridiculous." Mom pursed her lips and looked disgusted.

See what I mean? Lame.

Thankfully, Deputy Hotstuff chose that moment to make his appearance.

Mom rushed over and did her whole clutching-and-hugging routine again. Deputy Hotstuff looked severely embarrassed. I didn't blame him. Mom got lipstick all over his shoulder. (I don't think he noticed, though. Not then, anyway.)

Then Mom got all serious. "Where's Sheriff Shifflett? There's been a serious crime here."

I heard giggling from my backpack. I tried to do that cough routine to cover it, so I'm not sure if anyone noticed.

Deputy Hotstuff looked even more embarrassed. He may be a deputy, but he's just out of school—only a year or two older than Tina, so he hardly qualifies as a full-fledged grown-up. (Or at least that's what I think Mom was implying. I may be projecting here.)

"He's out of town? At the Governor's Conference? He's collecting an award for the Knoble arrests. But don't worry, ma'am, I've got everything under control here. They wouldn't have sent me otherwise."

I have to say, if you're trying to sound official and grown up, it's probably a good idea to make sure your voice doesn't crack when you're talking. Oh, and that making every sentence a question thing? Not so adult-sounding either. But that's just my opinion.

"Well, you should take lots of notes for him then. And do you have a camera? You'll need to document everything with photos." I don't know if Mom really thought that a photo of an empty place on the counter would be helpful, but heck, I wasn't arguing. Mom grabbed Deputy Ben by the shoulder and dragged him into the kitchen to show him the place where Eunice and Harold used to hang out, I guess. I made my escape upstairs to hide evidence.

I made sure the door was shut tight before I unzipped my bag. The knickknack crew came out, looking more sheepish than usual. Even with the door shut, I could hear Mom downstairs. She was using her shrieky hysterical voice. I caught the "left to me by my grandmother" line again. When she gets upset, Mom tends to turn into a broken record.

The china dog blushed and cleared his throat. "Nice lady, Grandma." He looked at the floor awkwardly.

Good to know.

"You guys are going to have to stay out of sight. And I mean way out of sight. Got it?" Thank goodness Fred hadn't come along too.

Eunice nodded seriously. "Or you'll go to jail."

Way to overstate the case, Eunice. The last thing I needed was a couple of shakers making me more paranoid than I already was. "Well, sort of." I hoped she wasn't right.

"Slammer for you. I've seen the movies. We'll stay out of sight." Harold looked grim. They really weren't helping my mood here.

"Just get in the dollhouse and don't come out until I say so, okay? Please?" It's not a good sign when your future depends on a couple of china figurines. But heck, I wasn't above begging.

Eunice patted me on the hand with her little hoof. "We'll be quiet. But if you get a chance?" She did a little hip swivel. There was no sound at all from her insides. "I'm very clumpy," she whispered.

I nodded. "I'll see what I can do." Nothing like adding "find a good sheep innard substitute" to your list of things to do.

Eunice trotted over to the china dog. "Come see your room! I think you'll like it. Of course, we can always rearrange the furniture if you'd like."

"And there's a piano in the living room. Do you sing?" I groaned as Harold followed the other two into the dollhouse. Then I pushed the whole thing into the corner and hoped nobody looked at it too closely.

I hung around upstairs for a while before heading back down, basically doing your surreptitious peeking under beds and behind doors for rogue stone Egyptian cats. I came up with nothing, though. Which I guess was good, but it still made me nervous. I would've been happy to hang out upstairs all night, but two things got me shooting downstairs faster than a Roman candle.

One, I heard the door slamming as Bethany and Tina came home. (Which, okay, didn't really motivate me to go anywhere but into seclusion.) And two, I heard Mr. Boots doing his "Tina's home" scream (happy or terrified, it's hard to say which). That wasn't unusual, except this time it was accompanied by the shriek of his new sidekick, Squeak. Who technically shouldn't have been squeaking on his own, if you catch my drift.

I shot downstairs and slid into the kitchen, expecting a variety of expressions of shock and amazement, maybe Mom passed out on the floor, or Deputy Ben with his gun drawn. I definitely didn't expect them all to be standing around eating Mom's Velveeta crab dip. (Seriously, most people aren't that brave.) Nobody had that *Did that squeaky toy just move?* look of horror that I'd been expecting. (I did get a nasty glare from Bethany, who I guess has not learned to forgive and forget.)

I passed on the crab dip and started stirring a pot of whatever the heck Mom was cooking on the stove. Which looked like a big pot of water and crushed tomatoes. I'm thinking she hadn't been that far along with dinner before she noticed the sheep were missing.

There was no way we were going to be eating that for dinner, but I didn't care—the idea was to blend into the woodwork and stay under the radar. I scanned the room for Mr. Boots and found him under the kitchen table. He was wearing a gauzy aqua housecoat type deal, and he was openly frolicking with Squeak. And I mean openly. If they'd started a conga line around the kitchen it would've been more subtle. But I'm guessing it could also look like Mr. Boots was tossing Squeak around. You know, if you're brain dead or delusional or something.

I concentrated on my stirring, trying to keep an eye on Squeak while I avoided Bethany's evil eye. She was chatting with Deputy Hotstuff, but I could tell by the way she was crunching her Ritz crackers that she had it in for me.

It was almost worse than her actually saying something, that hostile crunching. Thankfully I didn't have long to endure it, because after a couple of minutes of crunch threats, Dad came home.

Mom rushed over, hugging, tears, kissing—you know the drill. Dad didn't seem the slightest bit fazed.

"That's terrible, hon. Have you seen today's paper? It's insane!" Dad said, throwing the paper onto the counter along with a big bag of Chinese takeout. Squeak squeaked and dashed between his legs, with Mr. Boots hot on his tail. Luckily Dad has a good sense of balance. "Thieves, all over town! Nobody's safe."

"Bill, hon, we have guests. You remember Tina's friend Bethany, and of course you know Deputy Ben," Mom gushed, momentarily going from Hysterical Mom mode to her best Donna Reed impression.

Dad nodded and shook his finger at Deputy Hotstuff. "You've seen the papers? What the heck are you guys doing out there? It's crazy! Do you even have time to eat?"

Ben blushed bright red. Even his ears were hot pink.

"First that pig, which I don't mind if they take— eyesore, if you ask me. But now thieves have made off with the lions in front of the library? Tell me, Ben, how can they do that without anyone noticing?"

I could've explained it, but Fred's "lions make great outfielders" line just didn't seem appropriate, no matter how true it is. (And honestly, who knows if it's even true. It could be some kind of lawn ornament urban myth.) I stirred harder.

Dad was on a roll, though. Poor Ben. He was doomed. At this point he could have gotten up and left and Dad wouldn't have noticed for twenty minutes. "What kind of operation are you guys running here, anyway? I'm not surprised thieves were able to just come in here and take whatever they wanted. Doesn't make me feel very safe, I have to say." He stared at Ben like he was waiting for him to apologize.

Ben cleared his throat. "We're on top of things,

Mr. Jacobs. I know it looks bad, but we've collected a lot of evidence. We expect to make an arrest soon—maybe in the next day or so. And I wouldn't be surprised if the same people who broke in here are involved."

Mom dabbed her eyes with a napkin. "I hope you catch them. That china dog was a family heirloom!"

Pretty mouthy for an heirloom, but I couldn't say that either.

"Is Shifflett the only competent one there? He leaves town and the whole place goes to hell?" Dad wasn't letting it go.

Ben swallowed hard. And noisily. I'm not kidding—everybody could hear it. "At least they didn't get your duck," Ben said, looking up at the top of the china cabinet where Tootie the garden duck's shrine was. It was an admirable attempt at diversion.

Tootie was just a regular plastic garden duck until earlier this year, when she caught the attention of the *Daily Squealer* tabloid and became a media darling. Then we had to move her inside to get away from all the groupies and gawkers. Mom made a little straw nest for her to sit on with display lights and everything.

I thanked my lucky stars that I hadn't thought to put the dragonfly on her, and that her display was too tall for Fred to reach. Tootie used to have a brother, Topper, who was decapitated by our neighbor's crappy driving a few years ago. I shuddered to think what the past couple of days would've been like if Tootie had been one of the things to come to life. I don't know if there are grief counselors for plastic garden ducks, but I didn't want to try to find one.

Ben's attempt to change the subject totally misfired, though. Mom looked up at Tootie and gasped. "Oh no, Tootie!" She started to tear up. "Do you think they'll be back?"

Good job, Ben.

"I'm sorry, son, but collecting evidence? That's not good enough. I need details, and I need them now." Dad slapped his hand on the counter. I heard Squeak give a little squeal.

"Dad!" Tina objected. "That's probably confidential." I was glad Tina had finally said something. I could hardly imagine Dad grilling Sheriff Shifflett that way. But I really don't think Sheriff Shifflett would've been stammering and blushing like Ben was either.

Now that the grilling session had turned into a Tina-Dad power play, I tuned out. Don't get me wrong—those are always fun to watch from the sidelines. But one of the newspapers Dad had brought home with him had caught my eye.

The *Daily News* wasn't so bad—its lead story was MASS HALLUCINATIONS GRIP TOWN—LOCAL CHEMICAL PLANT TO BLAME? CEO QUESTIONED which wouldn't get me cheering, but heck, it wasn't that bad, considering. It was the *Daily Squealer* that caught my attention, though. The headline KILLER STONE LIONS ON A RAMPAGE made it pretty hard to miss. I slid the paper closer. The other headlines weren't any more comforting. Apparently that stinkin' penguin had chased a woman three blocks and then mooned a whole movie theater of people watching the latest slasher film. The flamingos had been seen doing synchronized swimming routines in Lake Heather and the Macarena on Main Street, and it looked like those gnomes were keeping busy—mysterious garden repairs had been reported all over town.

The worst part wasn't even the headlines, though—it was the gossip column. "What well-dressed doggie has been seen around town with a new squeeze?" was the teaser. Like there was more than one famous well-dressed doggie in town. I glanced down at where Mr. Boots and Squeak were curled up under the chair. If the Squealer knew about Squeak, it was pretty much all over.

Mom brought the takeout into the dining room, so I discreetly wadded up the *Daily Squealer* and threw it into the trash. What they didn't know wouldn't hurt them.

Dinner was pretty much the hellish experience I'd been expecting. Dad went into sullen and silent mode, and Mom did a lot of nervous giggling (except whenever she seasoned her food—then she got all teary eyed over the plain white shakers we had on the table). Tina,

Bethany, and Ben were at the other end of the table whispering to each other, and I couldn't quite figure out what the deal was there. Apparently Bethany had given up on her destroy-Arlie vendetta for the moment and instead was doing a lot of hair flipping and arm squeezing. The arm's owner being one Deputy Hotstuff. Tina didn't look pleased.

I pretty much watched Squeak and Mr. Boots racing around the living room. There have been times in the past when I felt like maybe my family wasn't paying that much attention to me. And I always figured I was paranoid and it was all in my head. But what was happening with Squeak and Mr. Boots pretty much confirmed my worst suspicions. I mean, if you don't notice a squeaky toy drag race going on around your feet, you're a little lacking in the attention-to-detail department.

As soon as Dad put down his fork, Ben shot up like a jack-in-the-box and gave a half bow to Mom. "Sorry to rush out. Dinner was wonderful, Mrs. Jacobs. But duty calls, and as you know, I have a lot of work to do."

He was talking so fast, I was afraid he'd pass out, but he seemed to make it through okay. Dad just nodded grudgingly.

Bethany hopped up too. "Yeah, I'd better go too. Ben can give me a ride, can't you Ben?"

Deputy Hotstuff shot a desperate look at Tina. "Sure, no problem." Sure, not now. But later, hooboy, I bet it would be a problem.

"Thanks, Tina, this was great!" Bethany smiled as she swooped in for one of those back-patting airkiss hugs. Tina gritted her teeth and smiled back. I think I was witnessing the breakdown of the Bethany-Tina empire, but I wasn't going to stick around to be sure. I took the huggy good-bye session as an opportunity to sneak upstairs, discreetly pocketing a jar of candy sprinkles on the way. I figured they had to be an improvement over clumpy Tang.

The knickknacks were all asleep, so I put the jar of sprinkles next to the dollhouse window and called Ty on the cordless. I'm not naming names, but somebody obviously needed one of those nose strips, because they were snoring up a storm, and I couldn't hear a thing Ty said. So we agreed to meet down the block from Mrs. Wombat's house.

"So what's the scoop?" Ty said when I ran up huffing and puffing. It hadn't been easy getting out of the house—I think if Dad could post armed guards to make sure nobody would take our last remaining knickknacks, he would.

"They're close to making an arrest, according to Ben," I said. "I don't think he was talking about us. He may have been bluffing, though. Dad was pretty mad."

Ty nodded and pointed to Mrs. Wombat's tree. "I scoped out the tree a little when Mrs. W went off patrol, but there's nothing else there that I can see."

"So no answers," I said grimly.

Ty just shook his head. I leaned against a tree. We were totally stuck, and I didn't think I could keep this up.

I heard footsteps coming up the street toward us, so

I grabbed Ty by the arm and hid behind some bushes. It was easier to catch my breath while in a squatting position, and the last thing I wanted was for someone to tip Mrs. Wombat off and have us labeled stalkers. Turns out, I didn't need to worry. When the person came into view, it wasn't a person at all—just that stupid pervy garden penguin. It looked like he was out for an evening stroll. When he passed by, he gave us a little salute and then waddled away.

"Ty, we have to do something. That's insane." I was starting to have a real hostility toward garden penguins. They didn't even make sense to me.

Ty threw his arms up in a weirdly angry display. "Fine, Arlie, sure! But what? What do we do? Just tell me!"

I groaned. Attitudinal Ty was the last thing I needed right now. But since he was here, I might as well go for it. "Ask Christie. Just ask her. Please?" I didn't see what else we could do.

"Forget it. I've told you." Ty's jaw was set, which was

never a good sign. I've seen him get that way when we're arguing over whose turn it is on Nintendo or something, and once he gets that look, you might as well hang it up, because he's not giving in.

Mrs. Wombat's street is apparently party central at night, because a car turned onto the road and started toward us. We ducked back down behind the bushes and waited. But when the car was just across from us, there was a huge roar, and the two library lions leaped out into the road. I don't mind saying, it scared the crap out of me. Apparently it scared the crap out of the driver, too, because he swerved and crashed right into Mrs. Wombat's recycling bin.

While the driver was trying to get out from behind the air bag, the lions slunk away into the shadows, snickering as they went. I think they even high-fived when they got into the bushes, but I can't be sure.

Ty rubbed his hand over his head a couple of times and then looked up at me. "Fine. Tomorrow. I'll ask her tomorrow."

CHAPTER 11

IN A COUPLE OF YEARS, I DON'T THINK THERE'S going to be any living with Ty. I'm just going by Christie's reaction to him here. If she's any indication, I'd better start looking for a new best friend now, before Ty's head gets too big for him to move.

It's like he was a pop star or something, that's how she looked when he stopped her in the hallway. I think she actually stopped breathing for a second.

Ty attempted a smile. "Christie, listen. Remember when you overheard me and Arlie talking about that dragonfly pendant?" I really felt for Ty. Every word was a struggle. I think if I hadn't been standing right behind him, he would've turned and bolted right there.

Christie nodded. "I remember. I asked my dad all about it." She batted her eyelashes. I think it was supposed to look cute and flirty, but it just ended up looking like she had something in her contacts.

Ty swallowed. "Yeah. That's good. Can you tell us about it? The dragonfly?"

Christie put her finger on her lips and pretended to think about it.

I rolled my eyes. Christie was emoting like we were in a silent movie, and I didn't have time for the dramatics. "Look, tell us what he said, okay? We need to know."

Christie totally ignored me and frowned up at Ty. "Here? I can't tell you here. It's so . . . crowded." She looked around like the school hallway was usually a secluded and peaceful glen, and she didn't know where all the people had come from.

"After school then? Can you tell us then?" Ty asked. You know he was desperate if he was agreeing to meet her after school.

Christie attempted to flip her hair, but she was less than successful. She totally whacked Donna Cavillari coming out of the classroom behind her. Christie may have the fashion sense of a colorblind gnat on crack, but it was pretty obvious she'd been taking flirting tips from somebody. Judging from her technique, I'd guess hoochie mama music videos.

"I think I'm free after school." Christie smiled. "I can meet you then, Ty. Why don't you come to my place?"

"Great. We'll see you there." I grabbed Ty's arm to drag him away, but Christie just stared at me, so I felt the need to clarify. "I'm coming too, you know."

"Oh, no problem, Arlie. I totally get it." I wished she'd just talk like a normal person sometimes. I almost asked her just what it was that she got, but I held my tongue.

She nodded again. "So you'll be chaperoning the date."

Ty shook his head. "It's not a date. We're just meeting. To talk. We're hanging out."

Christie smirked. "Okay, sure. It's not a date. And Arlie's not the chaperone. We're just going someplace 'quiet' so we can 'talk.'"

Man, air quotes really bug me, and Christie's were the worst. I started wondering if Ty wasn't right about this whole thing.

By the end of the day, I was pretty much convinced of it. We'd talked to Christie after lunch, and in the span of a few hours, she'd managed to get word to the entire junior-senior high that she and Ty were dating. I don't know what was worse—all the elbowing in the ribs and high-fiving that Ty was getting from the guys, or the sympathetic looks that I was getting from the girls. Seriously, after this is all over, I'm having a T-shirt made that says WE'RE JUST FRIENDS in huge neon letters.

"Thanks, Arlie," Ty said through gritted teeth as we stood looking at Christie's front door. "Excellent advice. Just ask her, you said. How bad could it be, you said."

There was nothing I could say. "I'm really sorry, Ty. I had no idea."

"Well, we're here. Let's get this over with." Ty marched up to Christie's front door. She opened it before he'd even had a chance to knock. I think she'd been watching from the window the whole time.

"Ty, Arlie, come in." She held the door open for us. I actually had to give Ty a little push to get his feet going.

Personally, I had an image I was keeping in my head that I was using as a motivator. Just a little something my overactive imagination had whipped up to torment me in the dark hours of the night. A vision of how things might be if we didn't get this fixed. An image of Fred on TV being interviewed by Oprah. I could not allow that to happen.

"So Christie, tell us about the dragonfly," I said as I propelled Ty through the door.

Christie smiled and held out a plate of warm cookies. "We have plenty of time for that. Cookie, Ty?"

She'd certainly done an admirable job of fixing up the living room. At least, I'm assuming it doesn't usually have soft music playing and candles lit on the bookshelves. Ty took a cookie and stuffed it in his mouth whole as he flopped into a chair.

We needed to move on this. "Look, Christie, let's cut to the chase, okay? We need to know about the dragonfly. Then we can hang out." Yeah, the last part was a total lie. I feel so guilty.

Christie sighed and sat down on the sofa as close to Ty as she could get. "Well, I asked my dad, and he actually couldn't tell me much. Dragonflies aren't very common."

I groaned inwardly. If this had all been a ruse to get Ty over here, I was going to be in the doghouse with him for a long long time.

"He didn't know about any? None, maybe in town here?" She had to know something, right?

Christie selected a cookie and took a tiny bite. She was obviously going for dainty and demure. "Well, he said there was one. But he saw that years ago when my grandpa owned the store. That's probably too old to be yours."

"No, it could be. What did he say?" I was trying to keep cool, but Christie was driving me crazy with her debutante act.

"Old," Ty chipped in, spraying crumbs onto the coffee table.

"What?" Christie scooched closer to Ty.

"Ours is old," Ty said again. "Real old." Quite the wordsmith, if I do say so.

"It's made out of some black stone, really really black and sparkly. But the chain is broken," I said. I hoped she didn't ask to see it. I really wished Fred hadn't sewn it up inside her skull.

"Oh, okay. Well, that sounds right, actually. It's too bad you only have part of it though."

The temperature in the room seemed to drop thirty degrees. I wouldn't have been surprised to see ice crystals forming on the furniture. I didn't trust my voice to work, but somebody had to ask. And Ty's voice seemed to set on monosyllabic right now. "What do you mean, part?"

Christie smiled. "Well, the one my dad saw was in two parts—the black dragonfly is only half of it. There's a white dragonfly that made up the other half. They snapped together. Sort of a yin-yang kind of thing. Know what I mean?"

I totally knew what she meant. And I totally knew what it meant for us. We were totally screwed. No wonder everything had gone haywire. We only had half of the pendant. And I'd be willing to bet that without the other half, we'd never put things back to the way they were.

Ty seemed to have been doing the same mental figuring as me but he got his mouth working first this time. "So where is it, the other half? Who has it?"

Christie shrugged. "I don't know. Both halves disappeared like fifty years ago." She smiled. "Milk, Ty?" As if we could drink milk now. After she'd just delivered the worst news we could possibly hear.

"So that's it then. We've only got half." Ty stared at me with this dead look on his face.

"That's it then." At least Mr. Boots and Squeak would be happy.

I flopped back in my chair. I wasn't even trying to be a good guest anymore. As if I even was a guest. She hadn't even offered me a stinkin' cookie.

"Hey, guys, look. I don't know why you're so bummed. If you want to find out more about it, why don't you just ask? She won't bite your head off. That bones-in-the-yard stuff, everybody knows it's not true."

My ears perked up. "Ask who?"

Christie rolled her eyes like I was a moron. "The owner. Mrs. Wombowski. Gabriella Wombowski on Fletcher Street? She could tell you all about it. I mean, it belonged to her, right?"

Ty was up and at the door before I'd even processed what Christie had said.

"Great cookies, had a great time, thanks a ton, Arlie come on!" he called as he shot out of the house.

I scrambled to my feet and hurried after him. "Sorry, Christie, see you at school."

Ty was literally running down the street and there was no way I could keep up. At least I knew where he was going this time. There was no doubt in my mind he was heading straight for Mrs. Wombat's house.

Ty was waiting for me next to the skid marks from the lion-induced accident the night before. (I was going to say I caught up with him, but that is such a blatant lie. My running skills stink.)

"What do we say? Do we tell her we found it?" I said doubtfully. I couldn't just hand Fred over to Mrs. Wombat and tell her to do her worst.

"No, play it cool. We're doing a school project," Ty said confidently.

Ah, yes. The school project story. Almost guaranteed to fail, but it's our number one go to story. Hopefully someday we'll come up with a better line, but for now, we were going with it.

We did our fist-bump thing and marched across the

street. I have to admit, it kind of weirded me out walking into Mrs. Wombat's yard. It's like I expected land mines or something. And for some reason, all of her little stone animal ornaments were still completely inanimate, something that I wasn't used to these days. For a second I wondered why Fred and the others hadn't woken these up too but then I realized, duh, they didn't want to get a potato smack in the kisser. I just hoped we wouldn't.

We kept marching right up the walkway and onto Mrs. Wombat's porch, and without even hesitating, Ty rang the bell. Just like that, like it was any other house. I was pretty impressed.

I would've been more impressed if somebody had actually answered, but hey. We rang the bell again. No response. I have to say, some of my confidence was wearing off. It's not like we didn't know she was home. The woman never went anywhere.

"Bell's probably broken," Ty said, and thumped loudly on the door with the door knocker. There's no way she could miss hearing that. I'm surprised they didn't use that instead of the church bells, it was that loud and boomy.

We stood there like idiots for I don't know how long, until I heard a throat clear behind us. I'll admit it. I jumped about a foot into the air. (It's not just me, though—Ty did it to. We were startled, okay? Not scared. There's a difference.)

Deputy Hotstuff was standing right behind us.

"Hey Arlie, I'm really sorry." He did look sorry, actually, and I felt bad for him all over again. He was not having an easy week. "You guys have to move along now."

"What?" It took a second to get my voice to work. "Why? We want to talk to Mrs. Womba—Mrs. Wombowski."

"It's a school project," Ty piped up.

Deputy Ben smiled with his mouth, but it wasn't a happy smile. "School project, sure, I understand. But there's been a complaint. You're trespassing. Now move along."

He put his hand on his waistband just enough to show off his fancy handcuffs. It was a move I'd seen Sheriff Shifflett make, so I know what it means. It means move your butt or I'm throwing you in jail.

Ty wasn't ready to give up yet, though. "But . . ."

"There's been a complaint," Ben said again, nodding slightly toward the window.

That seemed to deflate Ty completely, like he was an inflatable snowman with a fast leak.

"Okay, we get it." Shoulders slumped, Ty trudged down the porch steps. I followed him, shooting an apologetic look at Ben.

Ty kept walking until we got to the Happy Mart and then he flopped down onto the Happy Hog's empty pedestal. "We were so close," he said.

I sat down next to him. The one woman who could help us was the one woman who'd rather shoot us than say hello. And there was nothing we could do to change that.

CHAPTER 12

THE NEXT DAY AT SCHOOL WAS NOT A HAPPY, fun time filled with sunshine and roses. Christie had switched from Ty worshiper to Ty hater overnight, and she wasn't above telling everybody in school how weird Ty was, bolting out of her house like a freak. Those were the words she used. And I came off even worse in her version of the story. I mean, nobody likes hearing themselves portrayed as a lovesick loser chasing after their best friend. (My best line in Christie's version was when I clutched my heart and shouted, "Ty! Ty! Don't leave me! I love you!" as he ran away in horror. I heard that part at lunch and it was all I could do to keep my tuna sandwich from coming back up.)

So you can imagine my joy when I discovered that in addition to all the psychological abuse I'd been taking all day, we'd be playing dodgeball outside in gym. I think I still have bruises from the last time we played, and that was two years ago.

I pretty much lack every essential skill you need for dodgeball—quick on my feet? Nope. Good at throwing? Nope. Popular or influential enough that people don't want to pound you? Nope. And guess who was on the other team? Bethany.

Thankfully, me and Ty employed our patented dodgeball survival technique of not moving at all, pretty much ensuring that we'd both be out in the first few minutes of the game. Sure, you get a nasty bruise, but you get to spend the rest of the time on the sidelines (pretending to be totally bummed out, of course).

So I was playing with a blade of grass when I heard

the sirens. I didn't pay that much attention at first, but when those sirens were joined by more sirens, and then more, and then even more, I knew something serious was up. (It's not like we have that many police cars in town, so if they're all going someplace, it's huge.)

"I wonder where they're going?" Marty Bollinger said as he took his shoe off and shook it out into the grass. Marty subscribes to the same dodgeball survival technique Ty and I do.

Ty figured it out a split second before me as we watched the police cars streaking down the highway behind the playing fields.

"Oh no, Arlie. They're heading out Old Orange Road. That means—" Ty stared at me in horror.

"Mandy." I jumped to my feet and took off running. Ty did too. (Marty did too, for a little while, I think in solidarity, but he dropped back when Coach Miller started having a freak-out.)

We were in our puke green gym suits and we were going to be in huge trouble, but that didn't matter. If those cops were headed for Mandy's house, they were going to find everything. Fred, Eunice, Harold—they'd all be busted. And it would be my fault.

I'd had delusions of getting there before the cops and sounding a warning. You know, your basic saving-the-day fantasy. But I knew I was fooling myself. They had cars, and as you're probably completely aware by now, I'm a crappy runner.

The whole street was blocked off when we got there and sheriff's deputies were milling around the yard, even some I'd never seen before. But the weird thing was I didn't see any lawn ornaments. Not one happy frog, not one dancing flamingo—that stupid garden penguin wasn't even there. And there was no sign of Fred or any of the others.

Ty and I hung back in the bushes to observe. Thankfully, our puke-green gym suits provided plenty of camouflage. I don't know what we thought we were going to do—maybe spring out and liberate a random lawn squirrel or something—but our hiding place in the bushes made it pretty difficult to see what the heck was going on. So it's not like we were actually doing anything useful except crossing our fingers. When the police cars finally started leaving, we'd been there for what felt like hours, and had only managed to get cramps in our legs and cricks in our necks.

When the last car left, we crept slowly up to the house and looked around. It was the weirdest thing. Mandy's yard looked completely wrong with all of the lawn guys missing. I hoped they weren't all in a holding cell somewhere trying to call us at home.

We'd started to make our way around back when Mandy launched herself at us from the side of the house. I guess she'd been inside and saw us through the window.

"They ARRESTED my MOM!" she shrieked, rushing at us with her arms flailing. "You guys, they arrested my mom! They said she's a thief!"

I felt horrible. This was worse than anything I'd ever done before. And the worst part was, I'd never seen it coming. I was so worried about somebody finding out what we'd done with the lawn ornaments that I never even thought about what would happen to Mandy if anyone found them here.

"What did they say exactly? Is she really under arrest?" Ty asked. I think he felt as bad as I did.

"I don't know," Mandy sobbed. "They said they'd gotten a call that she had stolen property, and they searched the place. And the worst part? All of our lawn stuff is gone."

I braced myself for the worst. "They took it for evidence?"

Mandy shook her head. "No, it was already gone. And the police wanted Mom to tell them where it was, and she didn't know."

"They don't have any evidence then? I mean, if she's innocent, she should be fine right?" I said that, but hey, I've seen cop shows on TV. I know how bad things looked for Mandy's mom. And I couldn't help but think about what Deputy Ben had been saying the other night. I had a bad feeling that Mandy's mom was the suspect they'd had their eye on.

"They kept asking and asking, where is it? And she didn't know. And I didn't tell them anything. I was afraid I'd make things worse." Mandy wiped her nose.

Something in Mandy's voice made me snap out of my guilt session. "You know where they are?"

Mandy nodded. "Fred, she saw my costumes, and she wanted to put on a show, right? But there's no place to put a stage here, not one that's big enough, anyway. So I told them about the old Hardy farm two fields over. It has a barn, so it's perfect. I think they must've gone there when they heard the sirens."

I took a deep breath. "You know then? About Fred?"

Mandy gave me a look like I was dumber than slime on the bottom of a fishbowl. "Yeah, Arlie, I kind of figured things out when I heard her griping about leaving her parasol at home. That kangaroo isn't exactly shy."

I could feel myself blushing. "Sorry I didn't tell you. I mean . . ."

"I did surgery on her head, Arlie. Kind of hard not

to realize she's alive when she's yapping about pain-killers." At least my stupidity was distracting Mandy from being sad.

Mandy wiped her eyes and sniffled. Better or not, we still needed some serious Kleenex around here, and fast. Thankfully, Mandy dug one out of her pocket. "Yeah, forget it," she said. "It's not like you had much choice. But what am I going to do?"

I took a deep breath. "First thing, we'll talk to the lawn ornaments and get the scoop. Next, I'll get Tina to find out from Deputy Ben how bad it is. And after that, I'm not sure," I finished lamely. As I'd been talking I'd figured out that I actually had no idea what to do. This thing had spun totally out of control.

"Uh, we're all fine, if that helps." Fred, the china dog, and the shaker twins peeked out from behind a rhododendron. "The others are fine too, but they're pretty mad."

"Nice outfits," the china dog snickered at me and Ty. Eunice glared at him, and he covered his mouth.

I've never been so relieved to see an orange kangaroo in all my life. "How did you get away?" I said.

Fred shrugged. "Those lions can move pretty fast. And flamingos can fly. Most of the outdoor ones can move it when they need to."

"Can we come back with you? Or will they throw you in the slammer?" Harold asked solemnly.

"Still crazy time over there at the barn," the china dog muttered.

I looked at Ty. The last thing I needed was to be carrying around hot merchandise, but there was no way I could turn them down. I put my bookbag down onto the ground. "Hop in guys."

The shaker twins and the china dog squealed and ran for the bookbag, but Fred shook her head. "I'll stay here, if you don't mind," Fred said. "I've got a ride."

One of the library lions stuck his head through the bushes. Those things never fail to freak me out, but I tried to look calm and collected. "Yeah, sure. No problem."

"We're going around town and getting all the stragglers. You know, meet in the barn for a strategy session. That kind of thing." Fred adjusted the plaid cap she'd swiped from Mr. Boots and hopped onto the library lion's neck.

I nodded. "We'll get these guys home." I looked at Mandy. "And we'll find out what's happening, I promise."

"Your Mom'll be home before you know it, I'll bet," Ty said.

Mandy gave a watery grin and turned and headed back to the house. I swung my backpack over my shoulder (more squeals—I swear I should charge admission. It's like an amusement park ride to them). Then me and Ty headed back into town.

With the exception of that crack by the china dog, I'd kind of forgotten that I was just wearing my ugly gym clothes, but boy, you remember fast when you start getting weird looks from people on the street. I'd never been so glad to get home in my life. But me and Ty had barely walked into the kitchen for some serious planning and snacks when there was a knock on the front door.

And when I opened it, I knew it was not a good situation. It was Sheriff Shifflett.

He's never been a happy camper around me, and this didn't look like the day that would change. His face was set, and he was looking grim. He took one look at me in my gym suit and it's like he knew everything that had happened.

"Arlene," he said. Just that one word, and I was a blinking petrified statue in the entryway. At least he'd figured out which Jacobs girl I was. That was a good sign, right?

"You're back?" I squeaked. "I thought you were at a conference. Congratulations, by the way. On the award and all."

"Gym suit, huh?" Sheriff Shifflett said, like gym suits were a crime. Beats me, maybe they are. "Three days, Arlene. Three days I've been gone, and I come back to this."

"Yeah," I said. Sucks to be him. Not a lot I could say though.

"You folks had some thefts here? Why am I not surprised?"

Well, I don't know what you say to that. So I kept my mouth shut.

Sheriff Shifflett took one step forward. "Now listen up, girl. I don't know what you've done here. But I've got a pretty good idea you're involved. Don't try and deny it."

It's true—me and Ty have been involved in some pretty weird stuff lately. I'd probably suspect me too. And as much as I'd like to say he is, Sheriff Shifflett's no dummy.

I made a strangled squeaky noise in the back of my throat, but Sheriff Shifflett held up his hand. "I don't want to know what happened. I don't want to know what you did. I just want you to fix it, you got that?"

He folded his arms and waited. And that was the precise moment that Mr. Boots and Squeak decided that the entryway was the fun place to be. They came racing down the hall at full speed, but when they caught sight of Sheriff Shifflett, they put on the brakes and came skittering to a stop. Or at least Mr. Boots did. Squeak, not being equipped with essential things like muscles or heck, let's be honest here, feet, wasn't so lucky. Squeak came streaking out and ran right into Sheriff Shifflett's leg.

Sheriff Shifflett looked down, Squeak looked up, and you can't blame the little guy for panicking. He gave a shrill squeal, hopped to his (for the sake of argument let's just call them) feet, and then raced back inside.

Shifflett didn't say a word, he just watched Squeak rushing back to Mr. Boots. Then he leaned in again. "Fix it," he said. Then he turned and walked back to his car.

I closed the door. It was all over. Sheriff Shifflett totally knew.

I went back into the kitchen where Ty looked as petrified as I'd been earlier. I don't think he'd moved from the second Shifflett had knocked on the door.

"He knows?"

"He knows."

Ty slumped down onto a chair.

Squeak made a pathetic strangled sound. I think it was supposed to be an apology.

"That's it then. We do what we have to do," I said. The idea had come to me as I walked back into the kitchen. We had no choice.

"What's that?" Ty asked.

"We break into Mrs. Wombat's house."

CHAPTER 13

YOU KNOW THAT LOOK THAT PEOPLE GIVE YOU
sometimes, maybe when they think you're off
your medication or a danger to society? That's
the look that Ty was giving me.

"Yeah, sure, Arlie. We break in. That way
Shifflett will have two reasons to arrest us." At
least I'd managed to snap Ty out of his stupor
and get him back to his cranky normal self.

"No, dipwit." I scowled. "Think about it for
a second, okay? This dragonfly is in two parts.
We've got one part. Who has the other part?"

Ty thumped his head on the table. "Not

necessarily, Arlie. We don't know that. You're jumping to conclusions." Ty could be such a spoilsport sometimes.

"But she probably has it, right? It's the logical assumption. The dragonfly pendant belonged to Mrs. Wombat. It's broken. We have this half, she has the other. It's sitting right there in her house! Probably. I mean, I guess."

Ty turned his head and just stared at me. I really didn't appreciate it. It was making me feel like a crazy person, and I don't like that feeling. It's much more fun when somebody else is a crazy person with you.

I couldn't take the staring, so to avoid the look of doom I picked up the *Daily Squealer* that Mom had gotten at some point during the day. I knew it had to be a new one because of the headline. DAY SPA ATTACKED BY HUGE HOG—IS NO ONE SAFE? Looked like the mudbaths had been completely destroyed by a crazed and overenthusiastic Happy Hog. I pushed the paper over to Ty. He looked at it and grimaced.

Finally he rubbed his head. "She's really old, right? Mrs. Wombat? She probably won't even hear us break in."

I nodded so hard, I thought my head would fall off. "Right! And it's not like we're really stealing anything— we'll just look around until we find the other half. And then we'll . . . something."

I kind of trailed off, because I actually had no idea what we'd do if we found the other half. But I did have an idea what we'd do if we didn't, which was (a) go to jail; (b) watch Mandy's mom go to jail; (c) get eaten by angry library lions (because you know they'll snap eventually). And none of those were possibilities I was willing to consider.

"And she can't keep that potato gun with her all the time, right? Heck, how much damage can a potato do?" I didn't mention the possibility that she had other non-potato-based weapons. Or motion detectors. Or an elec-trified force field with death-ray technology. The less we thought about this plan, the better.

"Right. So we go in tonight?" Ty looked about as enthusiastic as I felt, but it had to be done.

"Right! And we'll be right there with you," a tiny

voice piped up from my backpack. I unzipped it a little, and Eunice popped her head out. She shook her fists in what I think she thought was a menacing way. "She'll never be able to take the five of us. We outnumber her!"

I couldn't meet Ty's eyes. I had a terrible feeling we were doomed. The rousing knickknack battle cry emanating from the depths of my backpack didn't make me feel any better either.

It took some serious negotiating to convince those knickknacks that the best place for them was home at the dollhouse.

"But guarding the house is so boring!" Eunice wailed. Harold patted her on the hoof.

"It's for the best, Eunice. Remember what happens if they get caught with us?" Harold widened his eyes significantly.

"The slammer." Eunice sniffled.

"That's right. And they're probably going to be caught," Harold said matter of factly.

Gee, thanks, Harold.

"Probably? Ha! No probably about it! Those kids are toast, babe," the china dog chortled.

Gee, thanks, china dog.

Ty and I exchanged glances. This was not the support we needed. Especially since our actual plan was so lame. Basically what we had was ditch the knickknacks, wait until Mrs. Wombat went to sleep, and then sneak in. It doesn't take a brain surgeon to figure out the holes in that plan. (Heck, apparently you don't even have to be human.) I just figured that we'd deal with the problems as they came up, and not worry about them until then.

Problem one presented itself pretty quickly, and no, it didn't have anything to do with getting out of my house, which is what I'd been anticipating. (My not-worrying plan hadn't been working too well.)

Mom was still completely freaked out by the whole burglary thing, so she'd moved Tootie the garden duck into her bedroom and when they went to bed, I heard her barricade the door with something heavy, probably a dresser or something. I gave the knickknacks their millionth pep talk and even briefed Mr. Boots and Squeak about where I was going. Mr. Boots looked horrified, but had the decency not to say anything.

So I was feeling pretty confident when I met Ty across from Mrs. Wombat's house. At least until I saw the hammer in his hand.

"What's that for?" I hissed. Hammers weren't part of my plan.

Ty shrugged. "It's for breaking in? You can't break in without breaking things, Arlie."

Okay, sure, that made some kind of sense, but I hadn't been thinking that we'd actually break anything. I'd been thinking we'd find a well placed key under the mat or a conveniently unlocked basement door or something. "No way, Ty, we're not breaking anything. And if we bring that, we're armed! We're armed robbers!"

"So?"

"So don't think of this as a break-in, think of it as a sneak in and peruse, okay? We're just window shopping today. No breaking."

"Great," Ty muttered under his breath. He ditched the hammer by the tree. "But I'm coming back for it if this turns into more than perusing, okay?" He kicked at the tree grouchily. "She's going to catch us the second we set foot on her property anyway."

Way to think positively, Ty. The lights in Mrs. Wombat's house were all off, and I hadn't seen her do a quarter hour patrol, so I'm thinking she was asleep. We decided to give her another half hour, though. Not because we thought she'd pop out any minute, but because neither one of us was wild about what we were planning to do.

We crept up to Mrs. Wombat's porch, and when nobody ran out of the house screaming or arrested us, we regrouped. We'd already gotten farther than I'd expected.

"Now what?" Ty whispered. "Can you pick locks?"

Well, in a word, no. But I wasn't going to let that stop us. I crawled up onto the porch and looked under the mat. (No way was I standing up and providing Mrs. W with a big target.) Big surprise, the queen of paranoia didn't keep a key conveniently hidden in the most obvious place ever. And there wasn't one of those fake rock things around either.

"Hey, check it out." Ty pointed at the window by the door. "Is that open?"

I slid on my butt over to the window and inspected it. It didn't look open, and when I tried to jimmy it, it stayed shut tight. "No dice," I whispered.

"How about that one?" Ty said, pointing to the next window.

Remind me to sign Ty up for a tutorial in what an open window looks like. We did that sliding and trying windows routine all the way around the house, until I figured our only option was going to be Ty's hammer. And that was the last thing I wanted to do.

It wasn't until we were heading back to the front that we hit the jackpot. Hidden by the trees on the side of house was a little screened in patio. That's pretty typical around here, and if it's anything like the one at my house, it means the windows open in and are fastened shut with ancient rusty hooks. Hooks that tend to fall out.

I gave Ty a thumbs-up and pushed on one of the windows. It moved just the tiniest bit. I pushed harder, and the hook inside gave. So far, so good. I pulled myself up and slid on my stomach into the room. I felt something on my forehead, and I tried not to do the full-body shudder. I had a feeling I had cobwebs and bugs all over me.

"Ty, hurry!" I whispered. Ty was less graceful than I was—I blame his clunky sneakers for that one—but he managed to slide inside too.

I brushed off my pants and face (and indulged in a quick upper-body shudder) and looked around. We were in a tiny sunporch area, complete with wicker chairs with uncomfortable plastic cushions. Not a place I'd hide half of an ancient dragonfly pendant.

The door to the main house wasn't locked, so I pushed my way inside. My plan at this point was to start at the most likely place, which I had decided was the living room. (Okay, I know, the most likely place was really the bedroom, but come on, at night? With Mrs. Wombat in there? There was no way I was going in there.)

I crept through the murk of the house until I could see the streetlamps out front through the windows.

Ty poked his head into a door on the right. "Arlie—I think this is it."

We crept into the living room. So far, so good right? Every minute I didn't have a potato gun in my face was a good minute, according to my rules. I pulled my flashlight out of my pocket and switched it on.

"INTRUDER! INTRUDER! Oh wait, make that two. INTRUDERS! ALERT! TWO INTRUDERS!"

The voice boomed out overhead and it was the loudest alarm system I'd ever heard. Except I'd never heard an alarm system that modified what it was saying in a conversational tone. Which this one did.

It didn't matter what kind of system Mrs. Wombat had though—the cold, hard fact was that we were majorly busted. I looked around for a place to hide, realized what a dumb move that was, and then headed for the front door. Ty was way ahead of me, which is why he was the one who ended up with the potato gun inches from his nose.

Mrs. Wombat was in the doorway wearing a hot pink fuzzy robe with her potato gun. She did not look pleased. "What's going on here?" she demanded.

I opened my mouth to say something, anything, when a voice overhead beat me to it.

"They must've come in through the back. I heard them in the hallway and then they turned on a flashlight. That's when I woke you up," the voice said.

I looked around, but there was no one else in the room. Just me, Mrs. Wombat, and Ty, and we weren't talking.

"Are they thieves?" a tiny voice from down near the floorboards piped up.

Mrs. Wombat narrowed her eyes. "Don't know. Are you?"

I wasn't sure if this was when I was supposed to talk or not, so I didn't say anything. Mrs. Wombat seemed to be doing a fine job of carrying on the conversation by herself. Ty didn't seem to be capable of speech at the moment. He was mesmerized by the gun barrel under his nose.

"Well, I can't say for sure. I didn't see them touch anything," the boomy voice said again. I scanned the room quickly. And this time I managed to find out who was talking.

"Uh-oh. Busted. She saw my mouth move." The moose head over the fireplace looked embarrassed. "Sorry about that, Gabby."

My jaw dropped and crashed into the floor. "Did the moose head just talk?" I gaped at Mrs. Wombat.

"Great, Bruno. Good going. Now I have to shoot them." Mrs. Wombat looked serious, but she lowered the potato gun, so I tried to convince myself that she was kidding. Ty didn't look convinced, though—that barrel was still pointing at places he'd rather keep intact.

"Ha! I knew it'd be you! I knew you'd be the one to mess up. Not me! Not me!" The tiny voice piped up again, and I saw a turtle footstool dance across the floor.

I was beyond caring if I got shot at this point. I looked at Mrs. Wombat and Ty in disbelief. "Crap, Ty. Things here are alive." I turned to Mrs. Wombat. "Was Fred here? Did she do this?"

Mrs. Wombat propped her potato gun against the wall. "Who's Fred?"

"My orange kangaroo toy." I figured I may as well lay it on the line, since obviously a rubber room was in my future anyway.

Mrs. Wombat smiled for the first time (maybe ever in the history of the world, I'm thinking). "We need to talk."

CHAPTER 14

LET ME JUST SAY THAT I NEVER THOUGHT THAT one day I'd be having hot chocolate with Mrs. Wombat, her talking moose head Bruno and a maniacal turtle footstool. Just never entered my mind as a possibility. I still don't think Ty believed it. He seemed to be suffering from post-potato-gun-stress syndrome. It happens.

"So you found the black dragonfly?" Mrs. Wombat asked, taking a sip of hot chocolate. She seemed way calmer than I figured she should. "Was that you outside in the tree?"

I tried not to look guilty. "It was twisted up

on the branch. I didn't know who it belonged to."

Mrs. Wombat put down her cup. "I thought it might be caught on a branch, but I couldn't ever find it."

"What's with Mr. Chatty here? Does he talk?" The turtle footstool nudged Ty with his leg.

"That's not nice. I'm sure he's fine, right? Are you all right?" Mrs. Wombat actually looked a little worried.

"Have some cocoa, Ty." I put the mug in his hand, and he gave a weak smile. "He's just freaked out," I told the turtle, who seemed to accept that explanation.

"Do you have it?" Ty blurted out abruptly. "The white dragonfly, do you have it?"

Apparently Ty wasn't enjoying social hour.

Mrs. Wombat put down her cup. "I do. And I've been waiting for this day for a long time."

"Years and years," said Bruno the moose head wistfully. "Didn't think we'd ever find it."

"So where is it?" Mrs. Wombat clenched her hands together tightly, like she was restraining herself from lunging across the room and shaking it out of our pockets.

"We didn't bring it with us," I said. Mrs. Wombat visibly wilted. The moose head gave a low sigh.

"So we've been trying to figure out how it works. What happened? Why does the black dragonfly bring things to life?" I was going to make her give us the scoop if I had to take her footstool hostage to get it.

"And how do you make them go back?" Ty piped up. He still hadn't touched his cocoa, but he seemed to have some of his color back. I took that as a good sign. The turtle did too—he nodded at me and gave me the thumbs-up. Or he would've if he had thumbs.

Mrs. Wombat hesitated. "I don't know exactly how it works. I only know what happened. But it was a long time ago." She paused.

"Might as well tell them," Bruno the moose head said.

"I haven't heard this one in what, five minutes?" the turtle footstool chortled, stretching out and pushing Ty's feet up onto his back.

"Okay, short version. I was given the two dragonflies as a pendant—they fit together. The man who gave them to me warned that they were meant to be together and should never be apart, or terrible things would happen."

"He was her boyfriend," Bruno boomed. "But he was bad news."

"But romantic!" the turtle said. "Tell the romantic part. You never tell this part right."

"They don't need to hear that part," Mrs. Wombat said. She looked pretty uncomfortable. I didn't blame her. Fred had that same effect on me most of the time.

"He said that they were like the dragonflies, right? And that they should never be apart. He was blond, like the white dragonfly, and she had dark hair, get it?" The turtle sighed. "See, what'd I tell you? Romantic."

"Yeah, until the part where he ditches her for that hussy next door. How romantic was that? Huh?" Bruno sounded seriously annoyed. I shot Ty a look. I think we'd stumbled into a long standing argument here.

"Yeah, well I don't figure that part into my version." The turtle shrugged. "It's better without that part. Besides, in your version the guy isn't even a magician!

He's what, a traveling salesman or something?"

"He wasn't a magician!" boomed Bruno. "In real life, he was a traveling salesman. Can't you even get your facts straight?"

"Facts, smachts," the turtle scoffed. "I say he was a magician."

Mrs. Wombat cleared her throat. "As Bruno was so kind to point out, he ditched me. And I was angry."

"Sorry, Gabby," Bruno muttered, glaring at the turtle.

"I was in the yard when I got the news, so I broke the dragonfly pendant into two parts and threw them onto the ground. I didn't want to see them ever again," Mrs. Wombat said. "Later, I reconsidered, but when I went back into the yard to find them, I could only find the black dragonfly."

"This is the good part." The turtle nudged Ty in the shins. Ty smiled weakly. It looked like it hurt.

"I brought the dragonfly inside and hung it on Bruno's antlers."

"And it fell!" The turtle cheered.

"And it fell onto the turtle footstool," Mrs. Wombat finished. "The next morning when I discovered the two of them were alive, I was upset."

"She wasn't happy to see us." The turtle shook his head. "She did some screaming."

"I threw the black dragonfly out of the window, as far as I could." Mrs. Wombat took a drink of hot chocolate.

"Good arm." Ty looked impressed.

"Thanks," Mrs. Wombat said. "Too good, though."

"This is the sad part. Get ready," the turtle said mournfully.

"Poor Delilah." Bruno sighed.

"Delilah was my tabby cat at that time. She often went into the yard during the day. That day she went out and didn't come back."

The turtle sniffed mournfully.

"I went looking for her and eventually I found her," Mrs. Wombat said.

"She's skipping the squirrel part," the turtle said.

"Don't skip the squirrel part," Bruno said.

"Fine." Mrs. Wombat looked annoyed. "The yard was filled with stone squirrels, who knows where they came from, blah blah blah."

These three had been spending way too much time together, I could tell.

"Stone chipmunks, too," the turtle said.

"Stone hedgehogs. And bunnies," Bruno said.

"And when I found Delilah, she was stone too. With the white dragonfly hanging from her mouth."

The turtle shuddered, totally knocking Ty's feet off of his back. Ty spilled a little of his hot chocolate, but he covered well—I don't even think Mrs. Wombat noticed.

"Show 'em." The turtle waddled over to Mrs. Wombat and nudged her on the leg. "Go on, show 'em."

Mrs. Wombat got up and went over to a large locked cabinet. She put on a pair of white gloves, took a small key from a chain around her neck and unlocked it.

"Man, Arlie, we never would've found it," Ty said.

That last jolt seemed to have forced him into a full recovery. It was good to have him back.

Mrs. Wombat turned around, and in her hands she had a perfect stone kitten, with a translucent white dragonfly pendant dangling from a broken chain in its mouth. "Meet Delilah."

I shuddered. "That's her? That's your cat?"

Mrs. Wombat looked sad. "Unfortunately, it is. I think she found the pendant in the yard and was playing with it when it took effect."

"Man, that's creepy," Ty said.

Creepy doesn't even begin to describe it. The lightbulb went off in my head and I gasped. "Those stone animals out front? Are they . . ."

"Dragonfly victims, you got it," the turtle said. "Grosses you out now, doesn't it? Not so cute now, are they?" He giggled.

No wonder Mrs. Wombat didn't want anyone coming into her house or on her property. If I lived with a wiseass turtle like that, I'd be afraid of people finding out too. And the worst thing was, I was staring right into my own future. Because if we didn't get this all straightened out, I was going to be the one spending my days with a group of mouthy knickknacks for company.

"I knew someone had found the dragonfly when everything started coming to life." Mrs. Wombat looked at me accusingly. "You two made a much bigger mess than I ever did, though."

I blushed. It's not like we could deny it. I mean, she'd had the thing for years, and the Happy Hog had never attacked a day spa until now.

"So we've got both halves now, right?" I said, ignoring the guilt trip. "How do we make things go back? Do we clink the opposite dragonfly on them? Put the two halves back together? What?" Story time was nice, but we didn't have time for it.

Mrs. Wombat put the creepy stone Delilah on the coffee table and shrugged. "I don't know. I'm as much in the dark as you two. I'm hoping there's a way to put things right, but there may not be."

Just my luck to get teamed up with Mrs. Mary Sunshine.

Ty looked seriously ticked off. "Come on, there has to be something. Should we try the clinking thing? Since we've got the white dragonfly and these guys. We could click it against them and see what happens."

Bruno cleared his throat nervously. "I'd really rather not, if you don't mind. I like the way I am." He looked at us apologetically. "I'm just a head, see." He had a point.

The turtle jumped up and whapped his shell against the dragonfly in Delilah's mouth a few times. "Won't work, see? Believe me, I've tried it. Nothing happens." He was doing some pretty slick dance moves, hip-bumping that dragonfly pendant like that. Talk about disturbing.

Mrs. Wombat must've felt the same way, because she gently picked the turtle footstool up and put it down several feet from Delilah. "What I suggest is this . . . ," she started, but a muffled thumping at the front door interrupted her.

She instantly had her *crazy as a loon, paranoid-psycho-*

woman look on her face and grabbed the potato gun.

"Arlie? Ty? It's Fred! There's trouble!" Muffled thumping is the best a stuffed animal can do when it comes to knocking.

I grabbed Mrs. Wombat's potato gun arm. "It's just my kangaroo. They're okay."

I opened the front door and peered out. Mr. Boots was standing in the doorway with the strap to my backpack in his mouth. He had it slung behind him like a toboggan, and riding inside were Fred, Eunice, Harold, the china dog, and Squeak. They all looked completely freaked out. And even allowing for how scary a Chihuahua-led sleigh ride must be, there was still plenty of extra freaked out left over for something major.

"What's up, guys?" I went the casual route. If they were knocking on Mrs. Wombat's door, it had to be big.

"Thank God!" Fred hopped out of the backpack sleigh and stormed inside. "They're rampaging. Out of control. There's no reasoning with them. I figured we should come to you."

"It's your fault!" Eunice shrieked at Fred. "Tell her!"

"What did you do?" I had a sinking feeling in my stomach. It was starting to be a really familiar feeling too, and I didn't like it.

"Look, it was no big deal," Fred went on. "We were just in the barn talking. Just talk, okay? Just some lawn ornament strategizing. And I may have said a couple of things that got the others riled up."

"Riled up? Riled up?" Eunice squeaked. "They've declared war!" She was hopping up and down, and she'd obviously used the candy sprinkles, because she had a little maraca effect going on every time she jumped.

"Okay, maybe more than riled up," Fred said cautiously. "But it's not my fault."

"She told them that Cookie took her brain," Harold said, cutting to the chase. I appreciated his bluntness.

"And she told them what Mrs. Big Cookie said about lawn ornaments. That they're trash. And have no place in decent society," Eunice said, wide eyed with horror.

"That she'll be cleaning house and there won't be

any more ornaments once she's done," Harold said.

"It's not like that," Fred whined. "I didn't do anything."

"She said that Mrs. Big Cookie was the anonymous caller that got Mandy's mom arrested," Harold said, tapping his hoof on the floor.

"It was just talk," Fred wailed.

"She gave them Mrs. Big Cookie's address. And they're on their way there," Eunice sobbed.

I rushed to the window and pushed the curtains aside. The streets were filled with lawn ornaments of all shapes and sizes and they were all marching in the direction of Mrs. Big Cookie's house. Some of them I recognized, like one of the library lions and that penguin, but others were lawn ornaments I'd never seen before. And all of them looked angrier than I'd ever seen a lawn ornament look in my life.

I stared at Fred. I'd always been afraid she would go too far, but I'd convinced myself I was paranoid.

"We've got to stop them," I gasped.

Mrs. Wombat shook her head. "If you had the black dragonfly with you, we could try putting them together, but I don't think there's time to go get it. And we don't even know if that will work."

I looked at Fred. If we were going to try to put things back to the way they were, it was going to take a huge sacrifice on her part. And I wasn't sure how you ask somebody if you can take a pair of scissors to their skull.

"Fred can help," Eunice said. "Fred, do something."

"Give 'em the dragonfly, kiddo," the china dog said. "It's the right thing to do."

Fred sighed, pulled the waistband of her skirt down, reached into her pouch, and pulled out the dragonfly. "Sorry I wasn't straight with you. I took it out of my head when Mandy fixed me up. I was going to give it back eventually." She hopped over and pressed it into my hand.

"So now what, we just stick them together?" Ty said doubtfully.

Mrs. Wombat grabbed Delilah. "If we're going to try that, we should make sure we're close enough to the group. I don't want to find out too late that we were too far away. Come on."

She started for the door, but I hung back. I looked at Eunice and Harold, and suddenly I wasn't sure what the right thing to do was.

"But . . ." I stalled.

"What is it?" Mrs. Wombat picked up her purse. (Why she needed her purse, I'll never know. She was in a bathrobe, for goodness' sake.)

"What if . . . maybe they don't want to change back? Eunice, are you okay with this? If we put the parts together, you might go back to being salt and pepper shakers. Are you okay with that?"

I had a lump in my throat. Those guys had been the bane of my existence all week, but they were kind of cute, and heck, I was going to miss them.

Eunice cleared her throat and looked at Harold.

I'll admit it. I'd turned into a blithering idiot. "We

put these halves together and if we're right, everything will be back to the way it was. You guys, Fred, Squeak, everybody." I don't know why I kept repeating myself. I just didn't want to feel like a murderer, you know?

Squeak and Mr. Boots both gave squeals of horror and clung to each other. Then they took off, racing away down the street. Okay, too late. I felt like a murderer.

"Arlie?" Eunice said tentatively. "Don't take this the wrong way? Because it was fun visiting and everything, but heck yes, we want to go back! Harold, show her your hoof."

Harold muttered something under his breath.

"I don't care if it's embarrassing, show her!" Eunice demanded.

Harold stuck his hoof out. It had a small chip on the side.

"See that?" Eunice squealed. "Chipped! He stepped on a pebble and chipped his foot. Do you know how careful we have to be? One wrong move and we could lose a body part! Do you know the stress we've been under? We can't live like this! Please change us back!"

Harold and the china dog nodded emphatically.

"What she said," the china dog muttered.

"Oh." I felt pretty dumb, that's for sure. But at least I knew where things stood now. "Well, then let's change these suckers back."

Eunice let out a huge sigh of relief. "Thank you. Now get moving!" she squealed.

I loaded the knickknacks back into the backpack and Ty picked up the turtle footstool. (He didn't have much choice. What are you supposed to do when a footstool stands on two legs and stretches its arms out in the universal sign for "pick me up?")

"I . . . uh . . . I'll just stay here," Bruno the moose head said.

Mrs. Wombat went over and kissed him on the nose. "I don't know what's going to happen," she said.

Bruno blushed. "I'm thinking it's willpower. I'll be

here when you get back, and if I have anything to do with it, I'll be talking."

Mrs. Wombat smiled sadly and then marched to the front door.

"Let's get moving. I just hope we're not too late."

CHAPTER 15

LET ME JUST SAY, I'M NOT A PERSON WHO'S GOOD in crowds. The mall the day after Thanksgiving? Not my scene. So when we got to Mrs. Big Cookie's house, I was ready to whip out a paper bag and start doing my deep breathing. Because the whole block was crawling with lawn ornaments, and her house was the prime attraction.

Most of the time, lawn ornaments seem pretty happy, or if they can't manage happy, they go with brain dead. None of these lawn ornaments looked remotely happy. They looked seriously ticked off and ready to rumble. It was like they were reenacting the movie Frankenstein, and they'd taken on the role of the townspeople with pitchforks and torches. (I'm actually surprised they hadn't thought of pitchforks and torches—they would've been a nice touch.)

The library lions were on the front stoop holding a conference with a group of gnomes, a couple of plastic deer, and a lawn chipmunk. A plastic bear in overalls was behind them playing low dramatic background music on a ukulele.

Mrs. Wombat put an arm out to stop us from getting closer. It seemed like a pretty good idea to me, because I sure as heck didn't want to mix it up with those guys. I mean, most of them are made of hard plastic. That leaves a mark.

"There are so many of them," I said, trying not to panic. "Should we do it? Do you think they're all here?"

Ty shook his head. "Look around. At least one's missing."

I scanned the crowds. He was right. The Happy Hog wasn't there.

"Well, at least that's something, right?" I looked to Fred for confirmation, but she shook her head.

"Oh, he'll be here. It was his idea. Apparently he's got a bone to pick with Mrs. Big Cookie. Personal issues."

I didn't even ask for specifics. I was too busy trying to figure out if I might've accidentally slighted the Happy Hog at some point. Using his butt as a hiding place immediately popped to mind. I hoped he wouldn't recognize me if he showed.

The chipmunk on the front stoop started chanting something that I didn't understand. (I don't get chipmunks any more than I do squirrels. I think they talk too fast for me.) All the other lawn ornaments joined in and within a couple of seconds we had a full-fledged protest rally going on. Complete with random acts of violence. (The garden penguin pulling up handfuls of grass, flamingos doing something unmentionable to the bushes, that kind of thing.) If that's all they planned to do, I was fine with it, but it was pretty obvious that grass pulling was just the beginning.

"We need to move fast." Mrs. Wombat held her frozen Delilah statue out to me, along with a lacy embroidered handkerchief. "Just don't touch the white one directly. Use the handkerchief."

I looked down at the black dragonfly in my hand. "The Happy Hog's not here, though," I said doubtfully. I didn't want to get this wrong. If putting the two pieces together didn't work, we were out of options.

"Should we wait for him?" Ty said, watching the front stoop of Mrs. Big Cookie's house. The thumping of all the tiny plastic feet was making the ground vibrate. I really don't know how Mrs. Big Cookie was sleeping through it.

Mrs. Wombat pushed Delilah forward again insistently. "We don't have time to wait," she hissed.

I looked down at Fred, Eunice, and the others. "What do you think?" I said quietly. Well, as quietly as I could and still be heard over the thumping and the chanting.

"Well, if you ask me—" Fred started to answer, but suddenly the whole street went completely quiet. I looked around to see what had happened. Every lawn ornament was looking down at the end of the street. The Happy Hog was here.

He was coated in flaky mud from the waist down, I guess from the day-spa mud baths, he was wearing aviator sunglasses and had what looked like a cape draped around his neck. (I think it was actually a curtain though. Hard to say.) It was like the Happy Hog had gone on one of those makeover shows on TV and he was really working his new look. And, to tell the truth, he scared the heck out of me. Maybe it was because I couldn't see his eyes, but "happy" didn't seem to be the right word to describe him anymore. "Hostile" was more like it. And the Hostile Hog seemed like he could crush you with his hoof without a second thought.

The formerly Happy Hog muscled his way through the crowd of ornaments to a chorus of cheers and went right up to the front door. The library lions nodded at him approvingly and licked their lips. And then the Happy Hog lifted his fist and hit Mrs. Big Cookie's front door. Not like he was knocking, but like he was going to beat it down.

That sent Mrs. Wombat straight into overdrive. "Put them together! Put them together!"

I hesitated and looked down at Eunice. I wanted to say something meaningful, but nothing I could think of seemed right. And having to do it in five seconds wasn't helping either.

Eunice tugged my pants leg. "Put them together, Arlie. It's not good-bye. You know where to find us, and how to bring us back if you want. Just for a visit though."

Harold nodded. "Have some sprinkles handy. Eunice likes the sprinkles."

Eunice gave a solemn belly jiggle.

"Same goes for me, kid," the china dog said. "Except not the sprinkles part."

"Just keep me away from Cookie," Fred said.

"What is this, a sentimental journey? Just put the pieces together! Sheesh!" The turtle footrest squirmed in Ty's hands.

The Happy Hog thumped on the door again, and the sound of wood splintering filled the air. I grabbed Mrs. Wombat's handkerchief and peered at the two halves. Thankfully it was pretty obvious how they fit together, because I wasn't in any state of mind for major surgery here. I took a deep breath and clicked the two pieces of the dragonfly pendant together.

I froze, waiting. For a second it was quiet. I started to relax, but then there was another splintering crash followed by another cheer. Lights went on inside the house. Mrs. Big Cookie was awake.

"Well, that was anticlimactic," said Eunice. "I really thought it would work."

"Maybe they're not together right? We shouldn't have let the kid do it. I have doubts about her," the footstool said.

A cheer rose up from the crowd of ornaments as the

Happy Hog's fist broke through Mrs. Big Cookie's front door. The crowd of plastic animals pressed forward, eager to get inside. Another light went on in Mrs. Big Cookie's house. It looked like she was coming downstairs.

Ty looked at me wide-eyed, like he was ready to make a run for it. "What do we do now?" he yelled.

I shook my head. "I don't know!" I shrieked as the Happy Hog started pushing his shoulder through the front door. It was splintering like balsa wood.

And then suddenly, without warning, he stopped. For a second I thought he was just regrouping, and was going to let the ornaments go inside first, and then I realized they'd all stopped. Every one of them. They were just plastic lawn ornaments again.

It was like my legs gave out, and I sat down hard on the curb. Ty followed close on my heels, and then Mrs. Wombat was right there with us. Nothing else moved. And that's all that mattered.

The rest of the night was just a haze—lots of shrieking from Mrs. Big Cookie, who, I'm sorry, should count her lucky stars she's such a heavy sleeper. Because I don't even want to think about the shrieking she'd have been doing if she'd woken up a few minutes earlier.

Everyone in the neighborhood poured out on the street, staring at what was officially becoming known as an elaborate prank. Cameras flashed as people took pictures of Mrs. Big Cookie's yard. It did look pretty crazy, if you thought it was a prank—every lawn ornament in town was packed in so close to Mrs. Big Cookie's door that you couldn't walk between them. We knew it wasn't a prank, though, and the sight of that yard gave me chills. My parents saw me on the curb and just figured I'd come out like everybody else, so I wasn't even busted for sneaking out.

Police cars from three counties came screaming up the street, led by Sheriff Shifflett. He got out, scanned the scene and immediately started pushing back the crowds and cordoning off the area. He spotted me and Ty and for a second, I thought he was going to bawl me out, because he got this weird look on his face. Then he gave me the thumbs-up. It was just for a second, though, and then he put his business face back on.

"Awesome." Ty grinned at me and Mrs. Wombat.

I carefully picked up the china dog and the salt and pepper shakers from the road and put them into my backpack along with Fred. Ty offered the turtle footstool to Mrs. Wombat, but she shook him off—she had her arms full of a very squirmy and licky Delilah, who seemed very pleased to be unfrozen. Not to mention the garbage bag she'd filled with the white dragonfly's other victims when we headed out. Talk about a sack of stunned squirrels.

"Oh, yeah." Ty grinned at me. "It's over."

CHAPTER 16

WANT TO KNOW HOW BIG THIS WHOLE THING was? My street was still crawling with people when school let out, that's how crazy it was. The police released Mandy's mom first thing the next morning with an apology—they figured there was no way she could have had anything do with the assault on Mrs. Big Cookie's house since (a) she was at the police station at the time; and (b) she didn't even know Mrs. Big Cookie. (Sorry. Mrs. Saunders, I should say.)

Everybody in town showed up to gawk and see if they could ID their missing lawn ornaments. It wasn't all happy times, though. A couple of fist fights broke out. A lot of those lawn squirrels look a lot alike. Thank goodness Deputy Ben was there, making a note of everybody's claims and keeping the peace.

It was pretty cool to be able to sit out front and catch all the action, especially when Bethany showed up and started fawning all over Ben. Tina literally jumped over me to get next door. There's nothing like a good Tina-Bethany smackdown to make your day. Deputy Ben's no dummy either—he made it clear that his allegiance was to Tina, and so Bethany flounced back to her car, swearing that as far as she was concerned, the Jacobs family didn't even exist, which is fine by me. At least Deputy Hotstuff had the decency to look flattered and embarrassed.

As cool as that was, though, I couldn't help but feel a little gloomy. It wasn't going to be the same without Eunice and Fred and the other guys, and I didn't even want to think about what I was going to say to Mr. Boots. I hadn't seen him since he and Squeak took off. He was never going to forgive me.

"Arlie, I want a word with you," Mom said, coming out onto the front step. She was holding Eunice accusingly.

"What?"

Mom had practically cried when I'd brought them inside, so I didn't see what I could be blamed for here. I was the rescuing hero, right?

"Did you put sprinkles in here? It's a pepper shaker, Arlie. That's not funny. Your father got sprinkles all over his eggs this morning." Mom tapped her foot at me.

"Mom, I didn't do anything, I just found them. Whoever took them must've done it." I put on my innocent face and hoped she bought it.

"Oh. Right." She went back inside. Don't even get me started about how gross it is that my dad would sprinkle pepper on his eggs from a stolen pepper shaker without even changing it first. Personally, I don't think I'll ever be able to season my food with either Eunice or Harold again. It would just be too weird.

I looked back at Mrs. Big Cookie's house. A couple of people I didn't know were arguing over one of the pink flamingos, and Mrs. Big Cookie was being interviewed for some TV show. A truck had come earlier and hauled the Happy Hog away. They're planning on putting him back in front of the Happy Mart, but they said something about encasing his feet in cement, like they're worried he'll skip out on them again.

A girl who'd been inspecting some of the lawn ornaments stood up and looked around nervously. I groaned. It was Christie. The lawn ornaments weren't even a good cover. It was so obvious she was here to get the scoop on me.

I decided to take matters into my own hands. There wasn't going to be any more mooning around over Ty or spreading rumors. This was it. Time for the truth.

"Hey, Christie," I said, going over to where she was

holding the garden penguin. It wasn't hers, but as far as I was concerned, they deserved each other.

"Oh, hi Arlie," she said. She looked embarrassed, like she and the penguin had been caught plotting or something.

"Look Christie, about the other day?" I tried to figure out the best way to make her understand.

"Yeah?" Christie blinked at me. This wasn't going to be easy.

"Uh. Me and Ty? Yeah, we're a couple okay? And it's secret. Super ultra top secret. So don't spread it around, or I'll know it was you. Got it?" Okay, so forget what I said about the truth. I was going for what I thought would work.

"Yeah, okay." Christie nodded and put the garden penguin back. "That's what I thought. I wish you'd just said though."

"Sorry about that." I really was sorry, just not for the reason she thought.

I headed back to my porch and sat down. There

was still no sign of Mr. Boots, and I was starting to get worried.

Ty jogged up and flopped down next to me. "So who's winning?" he said, pointing over at the flamingo fighters. They were still going at it.

"Beats me. I don't even know who they are," I said. "How's Mrs. Wombat? Ms. Wombowski, I mean." I needed to cut it out with this nickname thing. "Wombat" probably isn't something you call someone to their face.

Ty had gone to drop off the turtle footstool before coming over. "She's making Delilah sick with all the treats she's giving her. I've never seen a more spoiled cat. And she's got a ton of confused squirrels and rabbits wandering around her porch. Apparently they're not used to being unfrozen, so they're just hanging out there. It's pretty awesome."

I grinned. I'd have to go over later and check it out.

"Oh, and Bruno says hi," Ty said slyly. Like it was the most normal thing in the world.

I practically jumped out of my skin. "Bruno? Are

you kidding?" I know he'd said he'd stay alive, but come on. Will power?

"Just as chatty as ever. He's really cocky about it."

Bruno being alive changed everything. "Mom!" I yelled. I raced inside, almost slamming into Mom's Egyptian cat. She'd found it balanced in the tree in the front yard that morning and she was still confused about how it got there.

"Have you seen Squeak? Mr. Boots's squeak—have you seen him?"

Mom was in the kitchen washing Eunice out in the sink. I averted my eyes.

"Do you know where he is?" I said again.

"Arlie, calm down, do you mean Mr. Boots's rabbit toy? He was filthy, so I put him in the wash this morning. He should be out by now, though."

My heart sunk. If Squeak had gone through the rinse cycle, there was no way he was up and hopping around. Poor Mr. Boots. He was going to be more depressed than ever.

I peeked down into the basement. Mr. Boots was lying in front of the washer and dryer, just staring. He was hardly even moving, that's how depressed he was. His green gingham skirt was all bunched up around his butt.

I went down and sat down next to him. "I'm sorry, Mr. Boots. I really am." I patted him on the head, but he didn't even look up. His little shoulders just started heaving. I adjusted his skirt and tried to think of the right thing to say. But they don't make a "I'm sorry your Squeaky toy stopped being alive" condolence card, so it's not like I'm the only one with a lack of ideas.

Suddenly something shot out from behind the dryer and hit me in the chest, practically knocking me over. It would've hurt, if the projectile hadn't been small and fluffy and smelling just-out-of-the-drier fresh.

Mr. Boots rolled over, his little shoulders still heaving with tiny giggles, and lolled his tongue at me. Squeak made a muffled squeally noise that I think was laughter.

"Ha-ha, guys, funny practical joke." I couldn't

228

hide my grin though. I wasn't sure how Mr. Boots was planning to hide Squeak from my parents for the rest of his life. But if anyone could do it, it would be Mr. Boots.

DAILY SQUEALER

REVENGE OF THE HAPPY HOG: REASONS BEHIND SAUNDERS ATTACK REVEALED

Police still have no official explanation as to why hordes of lawn ornaments, led by that miscreant fugitive, THE HAPPY HOG, led an attack on the home of one MRS. ANNETTE SAUNDERS and her six-year-old daughter COOKIE.

But although officials have stated that Mrs. Saunders and Mr. Hog have no known connections, this intrepid reporter was able to uncover a series of incidents that may provide an explanation for the lawn ornaments' vicious attack on Mrs. Saunders's home. According to numerous eyewitness accounts, Mrs. Saunders and her daughter had a long history of antagonizing Mr. Hog. Both were seen on numerous occasions oinking at the Hog, making critical remarks about the Hog's weight, rubbing its belly as it stood outside the Happy Mart, taunting it with the pork-based Happy Dogs purchased in the Happy Mart and, on at least one occasion, actually putting a piece of Happy Dog into the Hog's open mouth.

Though the Happy Hog remained restrained at that time, Saunders's actions can be described as thoughtless at best and rage-inducing at worst. Said one witness, who prefers to remain anonymous, "If she tried to force a Happy Dog on me, I'd beat her house in too." (CONTINUED, PAGE 6)

RELATED STORIES, PAGE 4:

NETWORK EXPRESSES INTEREST IN
HOG MAKEOVER SHOW

FROZEN FOR YEARS, DELILAH REVEALS
SECRETS FROM BEYOND

GARDEN PENGUINS:
CUTE AND CUDDLY OR
UNNATURAL MUTANTS?

ALSO, PAGE 2:

MADAME OLGA'S WARNING:
MR. BOOTS
IN DANGER!

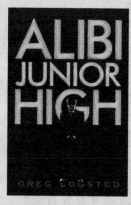